LAUGH YOUR HEAD OFF AGAIN

Pan Macmillan acknowledges the Traditional Custodians of country throughout Australia and their connections to lands, waters and communities. We pay our respect to Elders past and present and extend that respect to all Aboriginal and Torres Strait Islander peoples today. We honour more than sixty thousand years of storytelling, art and culture.

First published 2016 in Macmillan by Pan Macmillan Australia Pty Ltd
This Pan edition published 2022 by Pan Macmillan Australia Pty Ltd
1 Market Street, Sydney, New South Wales, Australia, 2000

Cataloguing-in-Publication entry is available
from the National Library of Australia
http://catalogue.nla.gov.au

Typeset in 11.5/17pt Charter by i2i Design
Printed by IVE Group

The paper in this book is FSC® certified.
FSC® promotes environmentally responsible,
socially beneficial and economically viable
management of the world's forests.

LAUGH YOUR HEAD OFF...

illustrations
by
Andrea
Innocent

PAN
Pan Macmillan Australia

A
G
A
I
N

CONTENTS

BUSTING

by

Andy Griffiths

I'm in the supermarket trying to remember what groceries Mum wanted me to pick up, but I can't think. I can't breathe. I can't do anything. I'm busting. And I don't mean busting. I mean BUSTING!

I've got to find a toilet. Fast. Then I can come back and think about the shopping with a clear head. Or not so much a clear head as an empty bladder.

I haven't got a second to lose. I run down the aisle and skid round the corner.

WHAM!

Straight into an old guy with a walking frame. He staggers forward and crashes into a stack of cans. They go rolling all over the floor. The old man is lying in the middle of them.

'Well, don't just stand there,' he says. 'Help me up!'

I reach down, take hold of his hand and pull him to his feet. Luckily he's not very heavy. I stand his walking frame up for him. He's muttering words I don't understand.

The store manager appears. I can tell he's the store manager because his pants are too tight. Plus he's wearing a badge that says Store Manager.

'What happened?' he says.

Before I can say anything the old man answers.

'This silly young boy knocked me over. It wouldn't have happened in my day. When I was young we respected our elders.'

'It was an accident!' I say.

'Were you running?' says the store manager.

'Yes,' I say, 'but I'm . . .'

'There's no excuse,' he says. 'I think you owe this gentleman an apology. Then you can pick up all the cans.'

'But I'm busting!'

'You should have thought about that before you started knocking people over and destroying my displays,' he says.

I get the feeling that I'm going to get out of here quicker if I just do what he says. I turn to the old man.

'I'm sorry,' I say. 'I shouldn't have been running and I hope you're not hurt.'

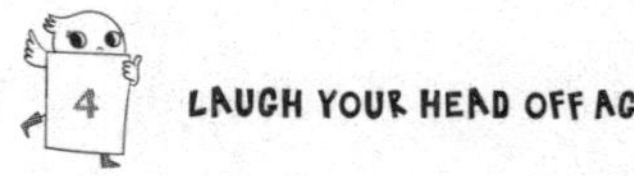

He shrugs and mutters something else that I can't understand. I start picking up the cans. I can't believe how far they've rolled. Some have rolled at least two or three aisles away. And the store manager makes me pick up every last one.

By the time I've finished I'm seriously busting.

But I know better than to run out of the store. This time I just walk very quickly.

I get outside the supermarket and into the main shopping centre. I'm looking for a sign pointing to the toilets. I can't see one.

There is a man selling pencils outside the supermarket.

'Excuse me,' he says. 'Want to buy a pencil?'

'No thanks,' I say.

'They're cheap—twenty cents each.'

'No thank you,' I say.

'Just one,' he says. 'One lousy pencil!'

'I haven't got time!' I say.

'You could have bought one by now,' he says.

'How many times do I have to say it?' I say. 'I don't want—or need—a pencil. What I need is a toilet. I'm busting!'

His shoulders drop. He sighs heavily. He looks like he's going to cry. If he's trying to make me feel bad then he's succeeding.

'Okay,' I say, fumbling for change. 'I'll have a pencil.'

I can't find a twenty-cent piece. All I can find is a two-dollar coin.

'Have you got change?' I say.

'No,' he says. 'You're the first one to buy a pencil today.'

'Keep the change then,' I say.

'No, that wouldn't be right,' he says. I'm not looking for charity.'

'Fine,' I say, 'give me ten pencils!'

He counts the pencils out really slowly, one by one. He makes a mistake and has to start again. I'm shifting from foot to foot.

Finally he hands the pencils to me.

'Have a great day,' he says.

'I will if I don't bust,' I say. I run off before he figures out another way to waste my time.

I'm running as fast as I can, but I'm not sure where to. I have no idea where the toilets are. This shopping centre is too big. There are too many levels. Too many people getting in my way. I want to scream.

I trip and stumble. I look down. My shoelaces have come undone. I hate my shoelaces. It doesn't matter how well I tie them up, they just keep coming undone. I can't ignore them, either, because they're extra long laces. Now I have to stop and waste valuable toilet-searching seconds doing them up.

I kneel down. It's not easy. It's putting pressure on a part of my body that's already under too much strain. I grab the laces and pull them tight. I loop them around each other. Then I loop the loops together and pull them tight as well. That should hold it. At least for a little while. I do the other shoe. I try to stand up. It hurts even more than kneeling down. I don't have much time.

Suddenly, hanging overhead, I find the sign I've been looking for. A picture of a man, a woman, a wheelchair and an arrow pointing to the left. I turn and sprint down a little corridor. I can see the toilets up ahead of me.

Oh no. I don't believe it. There's a yellow plastic pyramid outside the toilet.

Closed for cleaning!

Of all the times to clean a toilet, why now? Why not at night when there's nobody here?

Should I try to find another toilet or just wait?

I'll wait.

But I'm busting.

I can't wait.

But I can't not wait.

I have to go. Right now.

Why does life have to be so difficult?

Hang on! The handicapped toilet is not closed.

Can you go to jail for using a handicapped person's toilet when you're not really handicapped? Surely not. I'm sure nobody would mind. I'm busting so bad I'm practically handicapped anyway.

I hobble up to the door and push it open. It's vacant. I want to go in but something is stopping me. It would be so easy to just slip in here, and yet, so wrong.

If I get away with using this toilet, who's to say where or when it will stop? I could be taking the first step towards a life of crime. Today the handicapped toilets—tomorrow I'll be leaving my bike in the spaces reserved for handicapped drivers and walking up disabled access ramps instead of taking the stairs.

I can't do it. I let go of the door. I might be busting, but I'm not a criminal.

'Hey!' yells a voice. 'You can't use that toilet! You're not handicapped!'

I turn around. Oh no. It's the old guy with the walking frame. He's hobbling up the corridor towards me.

'I'm not going to use it,' I say, backing away from the door.

'Then why did you have the door open?' he says.

'Well, I *was* going to use it but . . .'

'A-ha! I thought so,' he says. 'Tearing around the supermarket and knocking people over. Using the handicapped people's toilets and stopping the truly handicapped from using them. You're a menace to society. I'm going to call a security guard!'

'No!' I say. 'I'm not a menace—I'm just busting!'

But the old man is not listening.

'Help! Guards! Arrest this boy!'

He's crazy. I've got to get out of here. He's creating such a racket you'd think he was being murdered or something.

I run down the corridor and back into the shopping centre. I'm not sure where I'm going. I need to find a location map.

I pass a shop with an enormous poster of a river in the front window. It's an ad for a video called *Great Rivers of the World*. If I don't find a toilet fast there'll be one more great river in the world. Right here in the shopping centre.

I can't hold out much longer. I can hear splashing. Uh-oh. I look down.

No, it's not coming from me. That's a relief. Well, sort of.

I look around. It's coming from the indoor fountain. There are about fifty thousand jets of water spraying in every direction. The sound of all that water is excruciating, but it does give me an idea. Maybe I could go in the fountain. I could get in, stand in the middle and pretend to be a statue. I could squirt water out of my mouth at the same time. Nobody will even realise.

But hang on! In front of the fountain is a map of the shopping centre. Fantastic!

I hobble over to the map. Hmmm. There are about half a million shops spread across three levels. So there are actually three maps. Lower, middle and upper with letters and numbers around the border of each one. It's very complicated.

And the sound of all that splashing is not making it any easier to concentrate. Whose idea was it to put a fountain inside a shopping centre anyway? I'd like to find that person and tell them they made a big mistake. And I'd like to find the person who made the shopping centre. I think they made the biggest mistake of all.

This shopping centre is way too big. I mean do we really need button shops? Or shops that sell nothing except stuff made out of cane? And as if there aren't already more than enough shops to buy gifts in, some genius comes up with the idea of a gift shop. As far as I'm concerned, the only thing more stupid than a gift shop is a shop that sells nothing but cat ornaments—and there's one of those here as well.

It doesn't help that the front of the map is suddenly smeared with water. I turn around. Two little kids are squirting each other with water pistols.

'Quit it!' I say.

They don't reply. They just squirt me. Right in the front of my pants.

There's a guy wearing a rainbow-coloured shirt standing next to me. He looks like a hippie but I'll ask him anyway. That's how desperate I am.

'Excuse me,' I say.

He turns towards me. His eyes are half closed. He looks like he hasn't slept for about three weeks.

'Can you help me find the toilets?' I say.

'Looks like it's a bit late,' he says in a slow voice.

'What do you mean?' I say.

He points to the front of my pants.

'That's not what you think it is,' I say. 'But it will be if you don't help me find the toilets.'

'Chill out, man,' says the hippie. He turns back

to the map and studies it carefully. 'Says here the toilets are at M 16 on level two.'

'What level are we on now?' I say.

'Ummm, level three,' he says, squinting at the map. 'No, hang on . . . level one . . . oops—make that level four.'

'Level four?' I say. 'There's no such level!'

'Hey, man,' says the hippie, 'open your mind. There are many levels. More levels than you ever dreamed of.'

'Are you insane?' I say.

'Relax,' he says. 'Take it easy.'

'I can't!' I yell. 'I'm busting! I've got to get to a toilet! Quick!'

'No man, you're missing the point,' he says. 'The destination's not important. The journey is where it's at.'

'Not when you're busting it's not,' I say.

I can't stand still any longer. I start running. I see an escalator going up. I jump on.

I don't believe it. It's almost too good to be true. At the top of the escalator is a sign. A man, a woman and a wheelchair.

I bound up the last few steps and leap off the escalator. Suddenly my leg is jerked backwards.

I look behind me.

My shoelace is caught in the top of the escalator! I try to pull my foot away, but I can't. The lace is in too deep.

I have to unlace my shoe.

I bend down and poke my finger in between the tongue and the lace. But I can't pull the lace out because the escalator has grabbed the other end of it as well. My finger is trapped.

The laces are being pulled tighter and tighter. My finger is going bright red. It's throbbing.

Great! Now I'm busting *and* I've got my shoelace stuck in an escalator *and* my finger stuck in my shoe.

I have to get my shoe off. I don't care about my shoe. All I care about is . . . well you know what I care about.

I put the index finger of my other hand into the back of my shoe to try to lever my heel out.

Oh no.

I don't believe it.

I can't get my finger out of the back of the shoe. The shoe is getting tighter. And tighter. And tighter.

The escalator is sucking. And sucking. And sucking.

There's nothing I can do, apart from chew my foot off. That's it! Chewing! Only I don't have to chew through my ankle . . . just my shoelace.

I bend right down. I'm trying to get close enough to the lace to take a good bite. All of a sudden my scalp starts burning. My hair is caught in the escalator!

This is like the most impossible and painful game of Twister ever. I'm bent over double, looking upside down through my legs.

Oh no.

The old man is coming up the escalator. He's got his walking frame held out in front of him. He's coming right for me.

He hits me fair and square in the bum.

I tumble forward. The shoelace has snapped and a huge chunk of my hair has been ripped out, but I don't care. I'm free!

'Now we're even!' shouts the old man.

'No we're not,' I say, scrambling to my feet, 'because you just did me a big favour!'

He looks dumbfounded.

I start running.

I'm almost there. Only a few metres more. Something is stabbing me in the leg. What is that? I put my hand into my pocket.

Aaaggh! Something jabs me in the thumb. It's those stupid pencils. They're too sharp. Like little spears. They could do me a serious injury in there. As I pull them out of my pocket they spill onto the ground in front of me. Uh-oh. Bad move. I'm going too fast to stop. I slip up on them and fall backwards. I whack my head.

Next thing I know I'm being shaken awake. I open my eyes. A fireman is kneeling beside me. The corridor is filled with smoke and I can hear sirens.

'Wake up!' says the fireman. 'Are you okay?'

'What?' I say. 'What's happening?'

He lifts me to my feet. I slip on a pencil and fall back down.

'You have to get out of here,' he says. 'Fire!'

He lifts me up again and starts shepherding me towards the exit. Away from the toilet!

I try to head back towards the toilet but he grabs me.

'Wrong way,' he says, pointing towards the exit. 'That way.'

'But I have to go to the toilet,' I say, 'I'm busting!'

'You'll have to wait,' says the fireman. 'It's not safe! You have to get out of the building.'

'Not safe?!' I say. 'If I don't get to the toilet soon, nobody will be safe. This shopping centre will be flooded!'

But he's not listening. He's escorting me to the exit.

Outside there are four fire trucks in a row.

The firemen are spraying enormous arcs of water onto the building. It might be helping to extinguish the fire but it's definitely not helping me.

I overhear the fire chief talking on his walkie-talkie.

'All we know is that the fire appears to have started in one of the escalators,' he says. 'Some foreign material may have got in there and shorted the system. Until we can put the fire out we can't be sure. But to do that we're going to need back-up units . . . as many as you've got.'

He wipes the sweat off his brow.

Suddenly I know what I have to do. I can solve my problem and be a hero at the same time.

'Excuse me,' I say, 'you're not going to need those back-up units.'

'What are you talking about?' he says.

'You've got me,' I say.

'Huh?'

'Watch this!' I say.

I go as close to the burning building as I can. I grab hold of my fly. I take aim.

Ahhhhhhhhhhhhhhh. Relief! Beautiful relief. The fire is powerless against me. It disappears in clouds of steam. People are gathered around applauding. The supermarket manager is there.

And the pencil seller. And the hippie. Even the old man. Cheering. Chanting my name. I don't know how they know my name but I don't care about that right now. All I care about is how good this feels. And how warm. It's so warm.

I roll over and snuggle down deeper into my blankets. My blankets? What are my blankets doing here? And why am I wearing pyjamas?

I blink a few times. I rub my eyes.

There's no shopping centre. There are no fire trucks. No people.

I'm in my bedroom. In my bed. Wrapped in my blankets. Putting out a fire. Only there's no fire either.

I hate that.

BEST IN SHOW

by

Frances Watts

'. . . and that concludes my presentation on burial rites for cats in Ancient Egypt.'

'Wonderful!' cried Ms Radish. She rose to her feet, applauding. 'Excellent work, Arthur.'

Arthur Ashenby, who was standing at the front of the room, smirked. 'Thank you, Ms Radish.'

The teacher turned to face the class. 'I'm sure you can see why I awarded Arthur the history prize,' she told us.

Ms Radish was right: I *could* see why she'd awarded him the history prize. It was the same reason she'd awarded him the maths prize and the science prize and the poetry prize and the geography prize—because Arthur Ashenby was the teacher's pet.

'And now I have some exciting news,' Ms Radish said as Arthur returned to his seat.

My friend Todd whispered in my ear, 'I bet Arthur has won another prize.'

‘Instead of our regular show-and-tell, tomorrow we are going to have a pet show. Those of you who have a pet at home may bring it to school. The best pet will win this beautiful ribbon.’ Ms Radish held up a blue rosette with *Best in Show* printed on it.

The ribbon was beautiful. I glanced over at Arthur Ashenby, who was eyeing it smugly. I knew what he was thinking: that blue rosette was as good as his.

What I would really like, I thought, would be to win that ribbon myself, just so Arthur Ashenby didn’t. All it would take was a really great pet. Something amazing and unusual; something no one else had.

There was just one problem: I didn’t have a pet like that.

In fact, I didn’t have a pet at all.

But I could tell by the look on Arthur Ashenby’s face that he did.

• • •

When I woke up the next morning, I remembered that I would have to watch Arthur Ashenby win another prize. I was feeling gloomy when I entered the kitchen for breakfast. But waiting there was the most brilliant surprise: a lobster! A real, live lobster!

Uncle Tim was watching proudly as it skittered across the floor. Mum was looking doubtful, while Dad looked dismayed.

'Thanks, Uncle Tim!' I said. 'How did you know I wanted a pet?'

Uncle Tim laughed. 'That's not a pet, Fergus,' he said. 'That's your dinner! I was down at the beach this morning and came across this fine fellow lurking in a rock pool. "There's a real treat for my favourite relatives," I thought.'

'But—' Mum began.

'But—' Dad started.

'No, no, you don't need to thank me,' said Uncle Tim. 'My pleasure comes from spreading light and joy among those I love.'

'But we can't eat it,' I said. 'It's *alive*.'

'It is now,' said Uncle Tim. 'But it won't be once you've dropped it in a pot of boiling water. Well, I'll be off then. *Bon appétit!*'

Mum, Dad and I stood staring at the lobster as it ran back and forth, waving its claws frantically, until at last it stopped running and stood on the spot, antennae twitching.

The three of us crouched down to look at it.

'We can't just boil it alive,' Dad said.

'Poor little lobster,' said Mum. Careful to avoid the claws, she reached out to pat it gently on the back.

The lobster's claws grew a little less frantic.

'Poor little lobster,' Mum crooned, still patting.

The lobster's antennae grew a little less twitchy.

'Poor little Lobby,' Mum murmured as the lobster drooped. 'Look,' she whispered. 'I've calmed it.'

Abruptly, the lobster sank to the floor.

'You've killed it!' I cried.

'I didn't mean to,' said Mum. 'What should we do with it now?'

Dad considered the dead lobster. 'Chuck it in the bin, I suppose.'

'No, wait!' I said, because I had an idea. 'Don't throw it out.'

'Why not?' Dad said.

'Because . . . ' It occurred to me that my parents probably wouldn't approve of me taking a dead lobster to school for a pet show; I had to think of a good excuse—and fast. 'We've been talking about Ancient Egyptian burial rites at school,' I said. 'Lobsters were worshipped in Ancient Egypt, you know.'

'Really?' said Dad. 'I knew the Egyptians worshipped cats but I had no idea they were into lobsters.'

'Oh yes,' I said. 'They've found heaps of mummified lobsters in the pyramids.'

'Huh,' Dad said. 'How about that.'

To my relief, he didn't question me any further.

'I think Ms Radish would be really pleased if I took Lobby to school for burial . . . for educational purposes. Can I?'

‘Well, I suppose if it’s for educational purposes . . .’ Mum said.

• • •

After breakfast, I put the dead lobster in a shopping bag and headed off to school feeling a lot more cheerful than I had earlier. At last I had my pet! Okay, so it was dead—but I would just tell everyone it was asleep. I was sure no one else in our class had a pet as interesting as a lobster. *Watch out, Arthur Ashenby,* I thought. *That ribbon has my name on it!*

When I entered the classroom, I saw that almost every desk had a cage or a box or a bowl on it, from which could be heard a fascinating assortment of growls and squeaks.

Ms Radish sat behind her own desk, beaming. ‘I’m glad to see you are all so enthusiastic about today’s show-and-tell. Arthur, why don’t you introduce your pet?’

The teacher always picked Arthur first.

Arthur took the cage from beside his desk, carried it to the front of the classroom and opened it. A nose emerged, followed by a spotty body.

We all gaped at it, trying to work out what it was. Finally, Ms Radish said, 'Er, is it some kind of rodent?'

'A rodent?' Arthur frowned. 'Certainly not; it's a marsupial.'

'Oh, of course,' said Ms Radish. 'It's a quokka.'

'Don't be ridiculous,' Arthur said. 'A quokka is a small marsupial that eats grass and leaves. This is a quoll, the second-largest carnivorous marsupial in the world.'

I groaned. There was no way my dead lobster could win over the second-largest carnivorous marsupial.

But to my surprise, Ms Radish didn't seem all that interested in Arthur's pet.

'Thank you for correcting me, Arthur,' she said. 'You and your quoll can step aside.' She turned to face the class. 'Who's next?'

'Me! Me!' said Todd.

Ms Radish nodded at him. 'Very well, Todd. Introduce us to your pet.'

Todd came forward, carrying a cage very similar to Arthur's. He opened it with a flourish and his pet sprang out.

'Not another marsupial,' the teacher said with a sigh.

'No way,' said Todd. 'This is Captain Squirrel!'

'But . . . isn't that a possum?' said Ms Radish.

'No,' said Todd. 'It's a squirrel. You can tell by the name: Captain Squirrel.'

'I see,' said Ms Radish.

Arthur snorted. 'I should think it was obvious even to the untrained eye that Todd's pet is nothing but a common brushtail possum.'

'It has a brushy tail because it's a squirrel,' Todd said.

'It's a possum!' said Arthur.

'Squirrel!'

'Possum!'

'Squirrel!'

'Enough!' shouted Ms Radish. 'Todd, you and your, er, squirrel may step aside.'

The teacher put her head on the desk for a few seconds then raised it again. 'Doesn't anyone have a nice, normal pet, like a kitten or a puppy?'

Jasmine Yu put up her hand. 'I do, Ms Radish,' she said.

The teacher smiled at her. 'Wonderful, Jasmine. Why don't you come forward and show us?'

Jasmine carried a cardboard box to the front of

MS. RADISH
TODAY: PET SHOW
BEST IN SHOW
RAAAA
SQUAWK!

the room, put it on the floor, and lifted out a tiny furry creature.

'That's not a kitten or a puppy,' Ms Radish said crossly. 'That's a baby fox!'

'Actually,' Arthur Ashenby said, 'a young fox is referred to as either a kit or a pup.'

'I didn't know that,' said Ms Radish.

'Why doesn't that surprise me?' I heard Arthur mutter to himself.

Jasmine put her fox on the floor and it immediately ran across the room and nipped Ms Radish on the ankle.

'Ouch!' said Ms Radish. 'That hurt!'

'She's only playing,' Jasmine assured her.

The teacher nudged the fox aside with her foot and looked around the class.

'Jessica,' she said, 'does that bird stay in its cage?'

'Yes, Ms Radish.'

'Good, you can be next.'

Jessica brought her cage to the front of the room. 'This is my budgie,' she said.

'That's not a budgerigar,' Arthur Ashenby scoffed. 'Anyone can see it's a blue-fronted Amazon parrot.'

'My budgie can talk!' Jessica announced, ignoring him. 'Come on, Polly.'

The bird squawked and then said in a voice exactly like Jessica's: 'Ms Radish is beautiful! Ms Radish is beautiful!'

Ms Radish blushed and said, 'What a wonderful pet, Jessica. Go stand with the others.'

The teacher surveyed the room, her eyes coming to rest on Aliya, who had a small shoe box on top of her desk. 'Aliya, you can be next.'

Aliya carried her shoe box to the front of the class.

'Actually,' she said, 'I don't have just one pet . . . ' She put the box on the floor and removed the lid. 'I have fifteen! That white one is Bernard, and there's Christine, and there's Hong, Alex, Fleur, Pookie . . . ' She was talking quickly as mice leaped and tumbled from the box. 'Cheryl, Humperdiddle, Princess, Nissan GT-R, Margherita Pizza, Taylor Swift and—'

I thought Ms Radish looked a bit weary as she said, 'That's enough, thank you, Aliya. We still have quite a few other pets to meet. Round up your mice, please.'

Aliya looked around the room. 'But I don't know where they've gone!'

We spent the next fifteen minutes rounding

them up, which got a bit chaotic when the quoll and fox and Captain Squirrel tried to help.

'I'm afraid we only have time for one more,' said Ms Radish. Her face was pale now. 'Hand up if you have a pet to show.'

I was so sure Jessica had won the rosette, I didn't even bother to put up my hand. But as usually happened when I didn't put up my hand, Ms Radish called on me anyway. 'Fergus Fairweather—let's meet your pet.'

Reluctantly, I picked up my shopping bag and took it to the front of the room. I put the bag on the floor and withdrew the dead lobster.

'This is Lobby,' I said.

'Why isn't he moving?' asked Jessica.

'He's sleeping.'

'Wake him up!' said Todd.

'Don't!' said Ms Radish. 'Sleepiness is a very desirable quality in a—ouch.' She glowered at Jasmine's fox, which had given her foot another playful nip. 'Now, what can you tell us about Lobby, Fergus?'

'He's a lobster,' I said.

Arthur Ashenby said, 'What a perfect pet for you, Fergus. Crustaceans are notoriously small of

brain—like you and your friend with the possum.'

'It's a SQUIRREL!' shouted Todd.

'And you're an IGNORAMUS!' Arthur shouted back.

'Squawk!' said Jessica's parrot. Then, in Arthur Ashenby's voice, it said: 'Ms Radish is an IGNORAMUS!'

'Arthur!' said Ms Radish. 'How dare you!'

'IGNORAMUS!' yelled either Arthur or the parrot.

'SQUIRREL!' yelled Todd.

'ARTHUR!' yelled Ms Radish.

'POLLY!' yelled Jasmine.

'LOBBY!' I yelled. Because my dead lobster had begun to move.

'Look, he's waking up,' said Todd.

'He can't be!' I said. 'He's dead!'

But Lobby was definitely alive. As he stretched a questing claw towards my nose, I quickly put him on the floor.

And then Lobby did the most amazing and unusual thing: he rose up on his many legs and began to skip in a circle. Then he raised his two front claws and twirled, antennae swaying gracefully, after which he danced swiftly and skilfully across the floor, his legs a blur of movement.

'Fergus,' Todd whispered, 'is your lobster doing *ballet*?'

'I don't know,' I whispered back. 'I think so.'

As the entire class watched in awe, Lobby continued to dance, dipping and twirling, spinning and leaping, until finally, claws and antennae raised, he jumped into the air once, twice, three times, then bowed.

'Bravo!' said Ms Radish, clapping loudly. '*Bravo!* That was magnificent!' She wiped a tear from her eye. 'I have never seen *Swan Lake* danced so beautifully. What an extraordinary pet you have, Fergus. Clearly you have a more poetic soul than I had realised.'

'Bravo, Lobby!' I patted him on the back.

The waving of his claws grew feeble.

'Well done, Lobby,' I said, giving him another pat.

The twitching of his antennae slowed.

'Good lobster!' I said, still patting.

Lobby slumped over.

'I've killed him!' I said.

'Of course you haven't,' said Arthur Ashenby in a superior voice. 'You were caressing its thorax. It's a well-known technique for rendering crustaceans unconscious. I thought everyone knew that.'

'No one likes a know-it-all, Arthur,' Ms Radish snapped. She turned to me. 'Congratulations, Fergus,' she said. 'You are the winner.' She handed me the beautiful blue ribbon.

As I gazed at the rosette in wonder, the teacher said, 'Is that the bell?'

'I didn't hear anything,' said Arthur.

'Well, I did,' said Ms Radish.

'But it's only eleven o'clo—'

'Quiet, Arthur. Class dismissed!'

• • •

'You're home early, Ferg,' Dad said when I got home from school in time for lunch. 'And you're looking very cheerful. The lobster burial went well, did it?'

'Um . . . yes,' I said. In fact, I'd stopped at the beach on my way home to return Lobby to his rock pool. It was the least I could do. 'And I won an award!'

Proudly, I held up the ribbon.

'*Best in Show*,' my dad read aloud.

'Isn't that an award for animals?' said my mother.

'Yes,' I said. 'That's right. I'm the teacher's pet!'

GREENHOUSE GAS

by

Morris Gleitzman

Today is a very big day for our family.

Me and Grandpa are both getting honoured. Grandpa's been voted Australian Of The Year and I've been voted Young Australian Of The Year. Plus we're getting a ten metre high concrete tomato. Nobody in our family's ever won anything before except scratchies so everybody's very excited.

But there's a problem.

Grandpa has jumped into the sea again and I'm out in the boat trying to find him.

'It's one-thirty, Grandpa,' I yell. 'You're being honoured in an hour and Mum reckons if you're not in your best pants by two-fifteen she's gunna get Andy Wicks to demolish the big tomato with his bulldozer and use the bits of concrete to build a new toilet block in the caravan park.'

I pause, out of breath.

All around me the calm surface of the sea

shimmers in the sunlight like a massively large plasma telly lying on its back. I used that description in my history project, but I only got six out of twenty.

I stare at the water.

I'm looking for bubbles.

Grandpa had fried tomatoes for breakfast as usual. When he goes snorkelling in the ocean after breakfast you can sometimes spot his gas bubbles. You have to make sure they're his bubbles, though. Once I tried to tell a big jellyfish it was morning nap time.

'Grandpa,' I yell again. 'Dad said to remind you that this is the proudest day in the entire history of our town, so try not to blow off at the ceremony.'

I peer at the sea.

'I'll try not to, young Dougie,' says a voice behind me. 'But my botty wind is the least of our worries.'

I turn around.

Grandpa is hanging onto the other side of the boat, treading water and pushing his snorkel mask up from his face.

'I wish you hadn't found me,' he says quietly.

I nod.

I know what he means.

I wish I hadn't found him either, not yet. I wish

I could stay out here for another few hours looking for him. I wouldn't even mind chatting with a jellyfish or two. That way me and Grandpa could both miss the ceremony.

Grandpa drags himself into the boat.

Sadly I help him.

We don't have to look at each other to know we're both feeling the same thing.

We don't want to be Australians Of The Year.

• • •

I row the boat towards the jetty.

'Careful, Dougie,' says Grandpa as we get into shallow water.

He always says that. It's because of the barbed wire fences just below the surface. This part of the sea used to be all sheep paddocks.

'It's OK, Grandpa,' I say quietly as I steer us past the roof of a submerged shearing shed. 'You can trust me.'

I always say that.

Grandpa usually smiles to himself and says 'yeah, I know', but today he doesn't.

He's frowning and concentrating on picking a

bit of seaweed out of his ear. I can tell he's thinking about things.

I know how he feels.

I'm thinking about things too.

'We'll have to own up,' says Grandpa. 'Tell them we don't deserve to be Australians Of The Year.'

My guts go tighter than a sheep fence when a shark swims into it.

But I know Grandpa's right. If we accept these

honours we'll spend the rest of our lives feeling guilty.

'If we confess,' I say, 'what'll happen to us?'

'Don't know,' says Grandpa.

Nor do I.

I don't want to think about it. Instead I concentrate on helping Grandpa tie the boat to the jetty.

'We'd better hurry,' I say. 'Mum's having a meltdown.'

I point over towards the house.

Mum's on the verandah, waving to us like an octopus stuck on a windmill. I used that description in my English assignment, but I only got seven out of twenty.

• • •

'Three cheers for Noel and Dougie Webber, the tomato heroes of Australia,' says the woman from the government.

There's a big crowd in front of the stage next to the surf club and they all give big cheers. Including my teachers, who still don't understand how a person who's never got more than eight out of twenty can be Young Australian Of The Year.

They don't have to worry.

I can't be.

I wish I could sneak off this stage and creep out of town and never come back. But I wouldn't make it. Hundreds of friends and neighbours are watching, and thousands of city folk from the caravan park.

Anyway, I can't leave Grandpa here to confess on his own.

The cheers die down, almost. Then Mum and Dad realise they're the only people still cheering and stop too. It's not their fault. They're just so proud. When they heard somebody was coming down from Federal Parliament House in Alice Springs to give us our prizes, they nearly cacked themselves.

I wish I didn't have to do this to them, but I do.

Grandpa, who's standing next to me, squeezes my hand.

'You OK?' he whispers.

'I think so,' I say.

The woman from the government is speaking into the microphone again.

'We may have lost the battle against global warming and melting ice-caps and rising sea levels,' she says. 'We may have lost our big cities, but thanks to Noel and Dougie Webber, we haven't lost the battle to feed ourselves.'

The crowd cheers again.

From up here I can see that heaps of people are having picnics and doing their cheering with their mouths full. I can see tomato pizzas and tomato sandwiches and lots of sun-dried-tomato burgers dripping with tomato sauce.

As the cheering dies down, I can also hear the faint sound of thousands of puffs of gas escaping from thousands of bottoms. It's what happens these days when crowds get excited.

And, to be honest, even when they don't.

'Five years ago,' says the government woman, 'a very clever little boy found something very special in his dad's paddock. A native Australian tomato plant that had never been discovered before. The boy's grandfather put its seeds into pots and, thanks to his skill as a gardener, got them to grow. And did they ever grow. They produced ten times more tomatoes per plant than any other type of tomato anywhere. And the rest, as we know, is history.'

I can feel myself blushing, partly because the whole crowd is clapping me and Grandpa, and

partly because in a moment I'm going to have to confess to a very big lie.

'Last year,' continues the woman from the government, 'Australia exported nearly a million tonnes of tomatoes to help feed the world.'

More cheering.

More gas escaping from well-fed tummies.

As usual, nobody even notices. That's the thing about botty gas. People start off being polite and pretending it's not happening, and then after years of ignoring it they don't even notice it anymore. Not even when it's erupting all around them.

Me and Grandpa notice it.

We notice it a lot.

Mum and Dad do as well, probably because Grandpa goes on about it when he's had a few glasses of tomato wine.

'It gives me great pleasure,' says the woman from the government, 'to unveil this monument to two very special Australians.'

Her assistant puts down his briefcase and grabs hold of the ropes attached to the big tarpaulin. He pulls on them and the tarpaulin slides down and ends up in a heap at his feet.

A bit like my insides.

That's what it feels like.

We all stare up at the Big Tomato. It's the tallest man-made structure in town except for the surf lifesaving tower, and it's definitely the brightest. Ken Bullock in the hardware store was mixing red paint for days.

When the crowd quietens down, as much as any crowd these days can, the woman from the government steps closer to Grandpa.

'And now,' she says, 'please welcome this year's Australian Of The Year, Noel Webber.'

She holds the microphone out to Grandpa, who doesn't even see it.

He's staring over at the shimmering ocean with a smile on his face, which is what he spends most of his time doing when he's not actually swimming or snorkelling. Mum reckons his brain might be a bit waterlogged, but I know that's not it.

Think about it. For the first sixty years of Grandpa's life, this town was hundreds of kilometres inland. Grandpa only ever saw the sea on telly. Now, thanks to melting ice and rising sea levels, we're a coastal resort.

Grandpa can't believe his luck.

None of us can.

We're happier than wallabies in wellies, which is a description I included in my science essay, but I only got four out of twenty.

I give Grandpa a nudge. He sees the microphone and takes it. We look at each other. Neither of us feels very happy right at this moment.

In front of the stage, lots of media cameras are pointed at us.

'Ladies and gentlemen,' says Grandpa. 'Thank you for your kindness, but I can't accept this honour. I don't deserve to be Australian Of The Year.'

People are gasping.

Bits of tomato sandwich are dropping from open mouths.

'We told a lie about where the new tomatoes came from,' says Grandpa. 'My grandson didn't really find a tomato plant in a paddock. What really happened was that I took an ordinary everyday tomato plant and did a bit of cross-pollinating in my greenhouse. Then I made up the paddock story so people would think the new tomato was natural and just as nature intended.'

The crowd has gone dead silent. All I can hear is the sound of the sea and the gulls and the gas escaping from multiple bottoms.

'We're sorry,' says Grandpa.

I nod to show I am too.

The woman from the government is looking a bit shocked. She pulls herself together and puts her hand on Grandpa's shoulder.

'We accept your apology,' she says into the microphone. 'The fact remains, you created a wonder tomato for the benefit of the world, and we want to honour you for that.'

The crowd applauds and whistles.

'Thank you,' says Grandpa. 'But there's another reason we can't accept this reward. It's hard to put into words, but every time somebody eats one of our tomatoes somewhere in the world, that's reward enough for us.'

I nod to show I agree.

The crowd is looking sort of puzzled. You know, like the eskimos when their igloos started melting and they knew they hadn't left the oven on. In social studies I wrote a letter to Iceland to say sorry, but when I showed it to Grandpa he made me tear it up, which meant I got nought out of twenty.

'I hope you understand,' Grandpa says to the crowd.

They just stare back at him.

I don't think they do.

Grandpa has been controlling himself very well so far, but now he stops clenching his buttocks and blows off big time.

I know what he's doing. Trying to give everyone a clue to help them understand.

The woman from the government is looking totally confused.

'Please,' she says. 'Just accept the honour.'

'Sorry,' says Grandpa. 'I'd rather not.'

'Me neither,' I say. 'It wouldn't be right.'

'But I don't understand,' says the woman, putting her hand over the microphone. 'You don't get any money from the tomatoes. What reward are you talking about?'

The crowd, which is frowning and muttering and giving off a lot of gas, obviously doesn't understand either.

I feel sick with nerves, but I take the microphone to explain to them.

'Our reward,' I say, 'is that our tomatoes make people fart.'

Some people in the crowd look shocked. But only because I used a rude word. They still don't get it.

Before I can continue, Grandpa takes the microphone from me and switches it off.

'Careful, Dougie,' he murmurs.

At first I think Grandpa means the rude word too. Then I realise what he's saying. We've done the right thing and confessed. No point getting ourselves in extra trouble.

'It's OK, Grandpa,' I reply quietly. 'You can trust me.'

• • •

I bite into a big red juicy tomato and sit back in my favourite chair, the cane one in Grandpa's greenhouse with the view out to sea.

I blow off, a long slow one that fills the greenhouse with a sweet tomatoey smell.

Grandpa doesn't mind. He's sitting next to me in his favourite chair doing the same.

He points down the hill towards the surf club.

'They're nearly finished,' he says.

He's right. The painters working on the Big Tomato have nearly finished painting it white.

'That was a clever idea of your mum and dad's,' says Grandpa. 'Turning it into the Big Golf Ball. When you've got the biggest caravan park in Australia, adding a beachside golf course is a top idea.'

Grandpa is right, it was a top idea. And a kind one.

A lot of the city folk in the caravan park need cheering up. It can't be easy, living in your four-wheel drive and spending all your time staring miserably at the sea and thinking about the place you used to live in that's now under water. Perhaps a bit of golf will help them feel better.

I hope so.

Grandpa has stood up and is pottering about up the other end of the greenhouse, watering his special plants. The onion weed and the kelp and the soy bean bushes and all the others. The ones he cross-pollinated with the tomato plants to get the side-effect he was after.

Grandpa's quite old and old people like to keep things for nostalgia. I'm young, but I know how he feels. We owe a lot to those plants.

Grandpa sits back down.

'Talking of clever ideas,' he says. 'Remember five years ago when the sea was still a hundred kilometres away and it didn't look like it'd ever reach us and all we had here was a drought-struck town full of dead sheep and unemployed people?'

I nod.

I'll never forget it.

Mum and Dad didn't have a job for the first six years of my life.

Grandpa's getting that misty far-away look in his eyes that old people get when they're having happy memories.

'Remember the day you asked me why the sea wasn't coming here any more?' says Grandpa. 'And I explained the ice had stopped melting because global warming was slowing down. Coal was running out and petrol was scarce and electricity was very expensive and people weren't making so much greenhouse gas and . . . what was it you said?'

When Grandpa's having these memories he likes me to say exactly the same words I said five years ago.

I don't mind. I know them off by heart.

'You've got a greenhouse, Grandpa,' I recite. 'Why don't you make some greenhouse gas?'

Grandpa stares out to sea with a big smile on his face and I know what he's thinking.

About the millions of people all over the world who've been eating our tomatoes for the last five years and blowing off.

I smile too because I know what he's going to say next and it always makes me feel happy. Even being Young Australian Of The Year wouldn't make me feel happier. The only time I feel happier is when I see Mum and Dad busy and content in their caravan park by the sea.

'That greenhouse gas idea was brilliant, Dougie,' says Grandpa. 'Twenty out of twenty.'

MR BIG AND ZIGGY

by

Katrina Nannestad

MR
FEATHERS

It was love at first sight, right there, in the middle of the City Shelter for Despised, Rejected and Neglected Dogs. The tan dog galloped across the yard, ears flapping, tongue lolling, and leapt at Ziggy. The boy tumbled to the grass for the dog was rather large. And when I say large, I mean enormous. To look at him, you'd think he was a mix of Great Dane, Labrador and horse.

'Woof!' said the dog, grinning and dribbling. He licked Ziggy's chin, cheeks and earholes and chewed two buttons off his shirt. Then, flopping to the ground, he rolled onto his back for a tummy tickle. He also made a very bad smell.

Ziggy stood up, waved his hand before his face and giggled. The dog leapt to his feet and pressed his wet black nose against the boy's white freckled nose. They stared at each other, eye to eye.

'Wow!' gasped Ziggy. 'What a massive doggy

you are. I think I'll call you Mr Big. Come on. Let's go home.'

• • •

At home, Ziggy and Mr Big played soccer, then sat side by side on the lounge, watching TV. At dinner-time, Ziggy shared his hamburger with Mr Big. At bathtime, he let Mr Big lie on the bathmat and eat the soap. And at bedtime, he invited Mr Big beneath the blankets and cuddled him all night long.

'This has been the perfect first day,' whispered Ziggy. 'We're already best friends. We'll have a super duper life together.'

Mr Big had to agree. Ziggy was a marvellous lad—generous, loving and not at all bothered by the foul doggy smells beneath the blankets. Ziggy's only fault, it seemed, was his lack of imagination when it came to naming his pets. Mr Big was a very dull name, especially when Mr Big had hoped he would be called something catchy, like Rocket or Horatio. Ziggy also had a fish called Mr Bubbles, a mouse called Mr Squeaks, a canary called Mr Feathers and a cat called Mr Whiskers. (This annoyed Mr Whiskers enormously because *he* was actually a *she*.)

The weeks tumbled by, a delicious blur of fresh air, exercise, food and love. Mr Big adored Ziggy and Ziggy adored Mr Big. But together, they developed a knack for getting into spots of bother—traipsing mud through the house, eating unsupervised cakes and pies, running through the flowerbeds, getting caught in the rain.

And sometimes, they found themselves smack bang in the middle of *large splatters* of bother . . .

The Great Paper-Eating Debacle

Mr Big had learnt a great deal from Ziggy since moving into the Johnson household six weeks ago.

'Sit,' said Ziggy and Mr Big would sit.

'Stay here and wait for me,' said Ziggy, so Mr Big would lie down and wait for Ziggy's return. Sometimes for many hours.

'Din-dins!' said Ziggy, and Mr Big would eat whatever Ziggy offered—pizza, cake, dog biscuits, grass, cardboard. It really was quite entertaining and Mr Big was glad to oblige, for he was constantly hungry and always got a pat or a cuddle for obeying.

On one particular evening, Ziggy sat at the dining table, staring listlessly at his first ever sheet of homework. 'This is so wrong,' he moaned. 'I've only been in Grade 2 for one and a half weeks.' His shoulders slumped.

'Woof!' said Mr Big, and he stuck his nose into Ziggy's ear. It was cold and wet, but meant to be cheering.

'Sit!' commanded Ziggy and Mr Big sat.

'Hmmm,' thought Ziggy, glancing sideways at

the hideous homework. 'Perhaps I can use Mr Big's obedience to my advantage.' He held the paper out to Mr Big and said, 'Din-dins!'

Mr Big ate the page.

Ziggy stared, blinked, then giggled. 'Good boy!' He gave Mr Big a tummy rub.

The following day, when the teacher asked Ziggy for his homework, he was able to say: 'Sorry, Miss. The dog ate it.' He did not confess that the dog had eaten it before he had even put pencil to paper, and the teacher, bless her trusting soul, never thought to ask.

Ziggy had found a winning formula. He completed no more than three lots of homework during an entire school term. The teacher sent home several letters of complaint, but Mr Big ate them before they reached Mr and Mrs Johnson.

This was all very satisfying for Ziggy. But, unfortunately, Mr Big developed an inconvenient appetite for paper. The mere rustle of an envelope or the swoosh of a turning page would set his mouth drooling, his stomach rumbling. He ate bills before they were paid, letters from long-lost relatives before they were opened and thrilling novels before the final chapter had been read.

On one particularly annoying occasion, Mr Big ate Mr Johnson's Annual Report the evening before he was to present it to his Board of Directors. Mr Johnson turned up at his meeting empty-handed.

'Where is your Annual Report?' roared Director Mills.

'Er . . . um . . . er . . . the dog ate it,' whimpered Mr Johnson.

'Ridiculous!' cried Director Samson.

'Pathetic!' scoffed Director Ascot.

'Make us all a cup of tea before I lose my temper,' growled Director Farnsworth.

So, Mr Johnson found himself in the kitchen, boiling the kettle, when he had hoped to be in the boardroom having his hand shaken and his back slapped. He had even dreamt of a promotion.

'Bad dog!' snapped Mr Johnson, the moment he arrived home. 'Wicked, destructive mutt!' He jabbed his finger at Mr Big's nose with every word. 'You ruined my day!'

Mr Big's ears drooped like a dead pot plant. His brown eyes blinked mournfully.

'He's just a puppy!' cried Ziggy, throwing his arms about Mr Big's neck. 'He doesn't understand.'

'He'd better understand,' grumbled Mr Johnson, 'or we'll be driving to the City Shelter for Despised, Rejected and Neglected Dogs.'

Oh dear! Mr Big gave up eating paper right there and then and Ziggy was doomed to complete his homework henceforth.

The Great Science Fair Debacle

Ziggy loved volcanoes. He and his father spent an entire weekend constructing a one-metre-high papier-mâche mountain, then painting it to look like the real thing. They hollowed out a large crater and planned to fill the top with bicarbonate of soda.

The day of the Science Fair arrived. Mr and Mrs Johnson and Mr Big stood proudly by Ziggy and his enormous volcano. They nodded kindly at the other competitors, even though the Lego Ferris wheels, ant farms, mould collections and homemade light bulbs looked inferior to Ziggy's life-like volcano.

'We're proud of you, Ziggy,' cooed Mrs Johnson.

'Best project here, son,' whispered Mr Johnson.

'Woof!' said Mr Big. He wagged his tail encouragingly and licked Ziggy's face.

The judges approached and Ziggy stood a little

taller. Mr Big sensed that something significant was about to happen. He planted his feet a little further apart and pricked up his ears.

Ziggy poured vinegar into the crater filled with bicarbonate of soda. His volcano erupted with a spectacular surge of white fizzing foam. Ziggy clasped his hands to his cheeks, rolled his eyes and let out a blood-curdling scream (he had been practising this all week). It was all very realistic and dramatic.

Now, Mr Big was a gentle dog, not inclined to snap or snarl, unless something took him completely by surprise—a balloon popping, for example, or an umbrella being suddenly opened indoors. As the volcano erupted and Ziggy hollered, Mr Big growled, leapt onto the volcano and snapped at the frothing lava, filling his mouth with bicarbonate of soda and vinegar. His teeth fizzed, his tongue popped and his gums overflowed. He spun around and around on the spot, howling and frothing at the mouth. He also emitted some shocking smells that made David Hitchcock's rotten egg gas experiment seem sweet and delicate. Finally, Mr Big leapt into the air, ran the full length of the hall, knocking children, chairs and model rockets flying, until he came to Jennifer

Robinson's Great Barrier Reef display. Diving headfirst into the fish tank, he gulped and guzzled the water until the froth and the foul bitter taste in his mouth had gone.

'Rabid dog! Rabid dog!' cried the adults, whisking their children to safety.

'My fish! My coral! My seaweed!' sobbed Jennifer Robinson. 'My beautiful Great Barrier Reef is ruined and my delicate tropical fish are traumatised.'

The Science Fair was cancelled.

'Bad dog,' scolded Mrs Johnson, over and over again as they hurried away, blushing beneath the glares of all the parents. 'Disgraceful, horrid dog!'

'You'd better shape up or ship out to the City Shelter for Despised, Rejected and Neglected Dogs!' roared Mr Johnson.

Mr Big bowed his head and snorted the last puff of white froth from his left nostril with a sigh.

'But it wasn't his fault!' wailed Ziggy, wrapping his arms around Mr Big's head and covering his jowls with kisses. 'He got a fright, that's all. He's just a dog and doesn't understand.'

'Well, he'd better understand soon,' snapped Mrs Johnson.

'Or else,' growled Mr Johnson.

Oh dear! Mr Big, innocent though he was of any malicious intent, decided that he had better be on his very best behaviour henceforth. He would not eat paper or anything else unless it was placed in his doggy bowl. He would not snap at surprising objects. He would not even make bad smells. He would do *nothing* that could lead either himself or Ziggy into trouble.

Unfortunately, events are not always under our control . . .

The Biggest Baddest Bother of All

One month later, a fluffy white Angora rabbit was introduced to the Johnson household. For three days, Ziggy looked after Mr Hoppity-Fluffity with great enthusiasm, giving him lots of fresh straw in which to sleep, clean water to drink and carrots to nibble. But Mr Hoppity-Fluffity had the personality of a pet rock, he scratched when cuddled, he pooped more than he ate and he had a very stupid name. (The name, of course, was Ziggy's fault, but there was nothing he could do about the dull personality, the scratching or the pooping.) Ziggy quickly lost interest and, a few days later, he forgot to latch the door on the rabbit hutch after tossing in a

bunch of carrots. Mr Hoppity-Fluffity escaped, dug a tunnel beneath the fence and took up residence in the neighbour's vegetable patch.

Meanwhile, Mr Big was being a model dog, playing nicely with his buddy, Mr Whiskers. Dog and cat were dear friends and spent a lot of time together. This particular morning they had eaten their breakfast side by side, chased butterflies around the backyard, snoozed together in a large wicker basket, then groomed each other in the sunshine. Mr Whiskers licked the hard-to-reach spots behind Mr Big's ears. Mr Big dragged his large pink tongue over Mr Whisker's back over and over again until her fur shone like a show pony's mane. Unfortunately, Mr Big ingested a great deal of long cat fur in the process and began to feel a little poorly.

By lunchtime, Mrs Johnson noticed that Mr Hoppity-Fluffity was missing.

Two hours later, Mr Big developed a dreadful bout of indigestion and started coughing up fur balls. You can imagine what Mr and Mrs Johnson thought.

'Wicked bunny guzzler!' screeched Mrs Johnson.

Mr Big whimpered and tucked his tail between his back legs, but that made him look all the more guilty.

'That dog must go!' roared Mr Johnson. 'First thing in the morning.'

'To the City Shelter for Despised, Rejected and Neglected Dogs!' shrieked Mrs Johnson. 'And he will remain there for the rest of his days because who would want such a bunny-eating beast in their home?'

Ziggy begged and pleaded. He threw himself on Mr Big's back, sobbing and howling, 'Ple-e-e-ease, Mother. Ple-e-e-ease, Father. Don't send Mr Big away. I love him. I will never find another friend like Mr Big. I'm sure he didn't eat Mr Hoppity-Fluffity no matter *how* guilty he seems.' (Ziggy had forgotten that he had left the door to the rabbit hutch open. His memory was appalling, but he was a faithful friend and trusted Mr Big, even though the evidence said he should not.)

'Enough is enough!' shouted Mr Johnson and stormed out of the room.

Mr Big was speechless. Of course, he was *always* speechless because he was a dog. But he was also downcast. He knew that he was in disgrace but he couldn't see why. Hadn't he been gentle, faithful and obedient? He slunk away to Ziggy's room, his body sinking lower and lower to the floor with every step until he flopped down onto the mat. Ziggy cuddled up at his side. The boy covered Mr Big's ears with kisses and drenched Mr Big's neck with his tears. Then he sobbed himself to sleep.

Mr Big did not sleep a wink. At two o'clock in the morning, he was wide awake when someone came in through the lounge room window and tip-toed around the furniture. Mr Big nosed Ziggy awake and, together, they crept along the hallway and into the lounge room.

'A burglar,' whispered Ziggy. He put his hand on Mr Big's back and said, 'Go get him, Mr Big. Chase him. Bite him.'

But Mr Big knew that chasing and biting people was wrong and he did not wish to further enrage Mr and Mrs Johnson. He had to be a good and gentle doggy. Flopping to the floor, he rested his chin on his paws and watched as the burglar crept from the china cabinet to the bookshelves, filling his backpack with the Johnson family heirlooms—an antique porcelain teapot, a gold fob watch, a crystal vase and five silver candlesticks.

Ziggy tugged on Mr Big's tail.

He poked him in the ribs.

He whispered, 'Ple-e-e-ease. Stop him.'

But Mr Big covered his ears with his paws.

Ziggy dashed into the kitchen, returning with Mr Big's bowl. 'Din-dins,' whispered Ziggy, and because he was an obedient dog and always hungry, Mr Big gulped the food down.

Yuck! It was salty and dry and clagged up his mouth. Mr Big gagged and shuddered and longed for a drink.

As though reading his doggy thoughts, Ziggy poured a whole bottle of liquid into the bowl and Mr Big slurped and gulped half of it before he realised it was not water, but vinegar. His gums fizzed, his tongue bubbled and, soon, his mouth was erupting like Mount Vesuvius. He leapt to his feet, yipping and yowling, white foam pouring from his mouth. He ran three circles on the spot then galloped into the lounge room, howling and frothing.

The burglar dropped his backpack, screamed in terror and scrambled to the top of the bookcase like a monkey up a tree. 'Help! Help!' he squealed. 'That dog has rabies. He's going to eat me alive. Get him away from me.'

But Mr Big howled and thrashed about, spitting and growling, snapping and gagging on the bicarbonate of soda and vinegar foam.

Ziggy ran back and forth along the sofa, waving his arms in the air, laughing and cheering.

Mr and Mrs Johnson came running into the lounge room.

Imagine their surprise when they saw a burglar on top of their bookshelf.

'Help me,' the intruder begged. 'I'm too young to die. Ring the police. Take me to prison where I'll be safely locked away from this ferocious hound.'

'Certainly!' cried Mrs Johnson. 'We'll be happy to oblige.'

'You stay right there where you're safe,' chuckled Mr Johnson. 'I'm calling the police right now.'

•••

The burglar was taken away and the family heirlooms were returned to the shelves. Mr Big was hugged and stroked and fed biscuit after biscuit until he could eat no more.

'You're the finest dog a family could ever hope for,' cooed Mrs Johnson, planting a kiss on his head.

'Faithful and brave and clever,' cried Mr Johnson, slapping him on the back. 'A real hero.'

'I told you so!' said Ziggy. 'He's my very best friend.'

'We will never send you away to the City Shelter for Despised, Rejected and Neglected Dogs,' declared Mrs Johnson.

'Never ever,' promised Mr Johnson.

'No matter *what* you do,' they both crooned.

A lesser dog might have made the most of such a promise and started to chew a book here, eat a rabbit there. But not Mr Big. He was a good, kind and loyal dog from the tip of his big wet nose to the end of his long tan tail. He enjoyed the rest of his days sharing Ziggy's bed, Ziggy's hamburgers and Ziggy's heart. He lived in peace and harmony with Mr Whiskers, Mr Bubbles, Mr Squeaks and

Mr Feathers. He even had the occasional good-natured chat with Mr Hoppity-Fluffity through the hole in the neighbour's fence. His only vice was that he stank, and nobody could blame a dog for that, could they?

THE SAUCERER'S APPRENTICE

by

Tony Wilson

My Grandpa taught me a lot about going to the footy.

He taught me which team to barrack for.

He taught me not to look down at other guys' thingies when we're at the urinal at half time.

He taught me how to avoid swearing by just saying the words 'shish keboob'. 'Shhhhish keboob . . . that wasn't a free kick!'

And, importantly for this story, he taught me about perfect footy pies. How to get them, how to eat them, what they mean.

Here is Grandpa's Pie Memorandum, recorded for future generations:

Memorandum for the Perfect Pie

- First, palm the pie, straight from pie warmer, and judge from temperature of wrapper if it's too hot or too cold.

- Next, unwrap and sauce pie. Careful! Too much and the insides become cold saucy sludge. Too little, and you can taste actual pie meat. Not a great idea!
- Next, return, with pie, to seat.
- Next, palm pie again, to reassess temperature. This is known as re-palming. Air pie, if required.
- Take cautious first bite.
- If pie is too hot, a little strand of skin at the back of your two front teeth will melt and dissolve and become one with the pie. Scream and say, 'Ahhhhhhhh too 'ot'.
- If pie is too cold, you'll feel the tepid sludge of something that might be meat sliding down your throat. You'll think to yourself, so this is what dog food must be like. Woof woof. Get me a bucket.
- If pie is perfect, you will know straightaway. Your only thoughts will be: How good is this pie? I have to have another pie. I have to keep eating pies until I have another pie as good as this.
- You will never have another pie as good as this.
- *Important* If pie is perfect, CONSUME IT AS QUICKLY AS POSSIBLE! Do not ignore this warning. Eating a perfect pie too slowly may endanger both pie and pie-eater.

My Grandpa taught me all of this and more. He gave me his Pie Memorandum for my last birthday, instead of a card. He wrote on the back:

Dear Pete. You may wait a lifetime. I had my last perfect pie in 1974.

I had a very good pie in 2014, although Grandpa doesn't think it was perfect. 'You'd be absolutely sure,' he says.

It's possible it was a fraction hot.

• • •

There was no sign on the day it happened that this was going to be my perfect pie. When I plucked it from the pie warmer, I said straightaway, 'Too hot'.

Grandpa agreed as we went through the pay station.

But then we re-palmed at the seat, and he was more hopeful. 'Maybe it just needs airing for two minutes; 2.10 at the outside.'

For pie novices out there, 'airing' involves exposing a segment of pie to the elements. Grandpa takes airing very seriously. He says he has an in-built airing computer that accounts for air temperature, humidity, wind speed, and whether the stadium's roof is open or closed. He always gives his airing recommendation to the nearest ten seconds.

'Good airing makes a terrible pie reasonable, and a good pie great.' How many times have I heard Grandpa say that!

I held the pie aloft for its airing. I figured the wind was stronger up above my head, which would cut down on airing time.

Grandpa was watching the footy, not the pie. He jiggled his right leg under his frayed old blanket. He stroked his neatly clipped white beard. He begged our players to lift. 'Shish keboob —' he hissed. 'When are our boys going to learn to kick straight!'

I was watching Grandpa, not the pie.

I was thinking about how much I loved going to the footy with him, because he was so passionate, and funny and—weird.

I was thinking about how my friends didn't really get him. Like the time I showed my best friend, Sol, the Memorandum for the Perfect Pie and Sol said, 'Why don't you just eat hot dogs?'

I was thinking how Dad didn't really understand him either. Dad wouldn't even read the Memorandum when I showed him. 'Don't tell me he's *still* going on about perfect pies?' he had said. 'Let me guess—you have to eat it really fast—*or else*?'

'That's right!'

'He used to say it to me, too. When I was your age.'

'Did you ever have a perfect pie?' I asked.

'1986,' Dad replied. 'Waverley Park. Although your grandfather didn't believe me. He thought it might have been a fraction cool.'

That had made me laugh. Grandpa was the best person to go to the footy with. He was the best person full stop.

I was thinking about all of this, with my pie in my palm and my hand raised on-high. It felt pretty good on the palm. Ready for eating.

And that's when it attacked.

• • •

It descended with an ear-splitting screech and a horrible flapping of wings. 'Crrrrrr, crrrrrr!' I saw a flash of black and assumed it was a crow, but then I saw white feathers too.

'Arrghhh, magpie!' I shouted. 'Grandpa! Swooping magpie!'

I ducked my head and retracted my arm, but the horrible flapping followed me.

'The pie!' Grandpa yelled. 'It's after the pie! Drop it.'

I flung the pie, and it narrowly missed the nose

of a little old lady sitting two seats up. But she barely blinked. She just stared at the game, her hands knitting furiously, noticing neither pie nor bird.

The pie landed face up. The bird was on it in an instant. It plunged its orange beak greedily into the pastry. Then it started sucking.

Its little white cheeks puffed in and out, in and out, like it was pulling on a thickshake. It had one dead glass eye fixed beadily on Grandpa and me. It made a horrible noise, which sounded a bit like Dad clearing his throat when he had a cold.

'Ughghghghh!'

'Sweet lord,' said Grandpa, clutching my forearm. 'It's him. He's back.'

'Who?' I said.

The bird raised its head and stared at us. Its orange beak was dripping with meat and sauce.

Now I saw it definitely wasn't a magpie. Its head and chest were ghostly white. Its wing feathers grey. And what I'd mistaken for black feathers was actually a tiny black cape, fastened at the neck. The beak had an oversized tip, like a giant orange tooth.

'Hello, Caarkula,' Grandpa said. 'I never thought I'd see you again.'

'Caaaaark!' said the seagull with the cape.

I clutched Grandpa's forearm.

'Is it a seagull?' I said. 'Is it a seagull with a cape?'

Grandpa nodded. 'It's a vampie seagull,' he whispered. They search the world looking for perfect pies and, if they find one, they strike.

That's why I said you have to eat a perfect pie quickly. You have to bolt it before Caarkula smells it.'

I looked at the smashed shell of my pie on the concrete of the aisle.

'That was my perfect pie?' I said.

'Must have been,' Grandpa said. 'Caarkula doesn't make mistakes. Did you get a bite?'

I shook my head.

Grandpa waved a fist at Caarkula. 'Demon!' he yelled fiercely. 'How dare you rob my grandson of his first perfect pie!'

'Second,' I whispered. 'I had a perfect one in 2014.'

'That was too hot,' Grandpa corrected. He tried to chase off Caarkula but the vampie seagull was unmoving. Grandpa stepped back, suddenly wary. 'Don't approach a vampie seagull unprotected,' he said quietly. 'That tooth at the front of its beak—it's razor sharp.'

Caarkula dunked his head back into the pie for one final slurp. 'Caaark,' he said, and then tossed his head back and laughed. 'Crrr, crrrrr, caaaaark!'

'Take it,' Grandpa hissed, almost under his breath. 'It's your pie. Take it!'

Caarkula clutched the shell of the pie with its

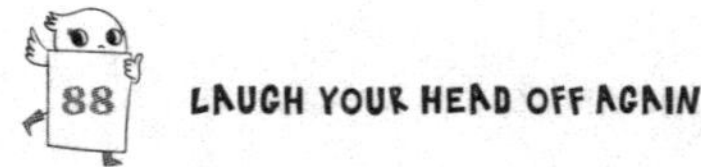

orange feet. Then he took off, white wings flapping, black cape trailing.

Grandpa grabbed his binoculars and spun around. 'Is he still holding the pie? Tell me he's still holding the pie?' The vampie seagull swooped and soared and then floated into the shadows of the members' stand.

'He's got it,' I said. 'He's still holding my pie. Is that good?'

Grandpa tossed his grey hat in the air and began a little dance. 'Yes!' he shouted. 'Yes, yes, yes!'

I was surprised to see Grandpa so ecstatic. Personally, I'd found the whole vampie-seagull-steals-my-pie thing quite traumatic.

'Finally,' Grandpa said. 'I've been chasing Caarkula for years, and finally, *finally*, I have my chance.'

• • •

Then, Grandpa shared an unpleasant truth about the pies I'd been eating. 'When you give them to me to assess temperature,' he said, 'I almost always slip in some homing gristle.'

'Homing gristle?' I said. 'What's that?'

'It's a tiny transmitter, disguised as gristle,'

Grandpa said. 'It can be pressed into the pie so I can track it. We know most vampie seagulls will take a perfect pie back to their lair. Homing gristle gives us the chance to follow them.'

'You mean I've been eating homing gristle all this time? That's completely yuck!'

'It's non-toxic,' Grandpa said, as though that explained everything. 'Besides. I had to. What did you want me to do, just give up on Caarkula? I can't do that. Caarkula is the big prize. I'm the Grand Saucerer.'

We exited the stadium and found a bench in the surrounding gardens. Sitting there in the fading twilight, Grandpa explained the great secret of his life.

'You see, Pete, there are only a few of us Saucerers left,' he said. 'We uphold the secrets of the perfect pie. We are engaged in the great struggle against Caarkula, and others like him.'

'There are other vampie seagulls?' I asked.

'Yes,' Grandpa said. 'Not so many as there once were. Particularly in pie countries, such as England.'

'And there are other Saucerers?' I asked.

Grandpa nodded. 'Your uncle Ned. He's a Saucerer. So's Ameet who works at the 7-Eleven.'

I thought of Grandpa's friend at the convenience

store. No wonder Grandpa took an age whenever we went in for Slurpees. He and Ameet had important secrets to discuss.

'What about Dad?' I asked. 'Is he a Saucerer?'

'Your dad?' Grandpa snorted. 'Of course not. Your dad's a scientist.' Grandpa sighed with disapproval.

We sat on the seat in silence.

'So do you want in?' Grandpa said.

'In for what?'

'Do you want to be the Saucerer's Apprentice?' Grandpa looked me in the eye and squeezed my hand. 'We Saucerers work together to track vampie seagulls and destroy them. But I have to warn you, it can get pretty hairy. Chasing vampie seagulls is not for the faint of heart.'

I felt a surge of adrenaline. My chest filled with a sense of purpose. 'Yes,' I said. 'I want to be a Saucerer's Apprentice.'

'Good,' Grandpa said. 'Well, prepare yourself because we roll tonight. Before Caarkula can find a new lair.' He cupped his mouth and shouted towards the sky.

'Tonight we come for you, Caaaaarkula!'

• • •

Ameet from the 7-Eleven came too. I wondered who was in charge of the store because I'd never seen anyone else behind the counter.

'Ameet, meet Pete,' Grandpa said. 'Pete, meet Ameet.'

It was a tricky name combination for introductions. What was even more confusing was that Ameet was carrying meat when we met.

Grandpa had given me the job of holding the steak sandwiches. They were hot, but cooling quickly in the wintery air.

'Have you got the safety pies, Saucerer Ameet?' Grandpa asked.

'Yes, Grand Saucerer,' said Ameet. He produced a dozen pies from a 7-Eleven bag. I read on the wrapper they were Lamb, Rosemary and Garlic.

'Do what I do, Pete,' Grandpa said. 'You place two safety pies in each of your jacket pockets. As close to the heart as possible.'

'Why?' I asked.

'They might save your life,' Grandpa said. 'Vampie seagulls don't like Lamb, Rosemary and Garlic pies. We think it's the garlic. It wards them off.'

Saucerer Ameet grinned. 'They hate these pies.'

I stuffed four cold pies in my pockets.

'Why don't you just use fresh garlic then?' I said. 'Pocketing garlic is a bit less messy than pocketing garlic pies.'

The Grand Saucerer and Saucerer Ameet began to laugh hysterically. 'Ah, Pete,' said Saucerer Ameet. 'They are called safety pies for a reason. They have to be *pies*.' They kept right on laughing, as if it was the best joke of all time.

This was turning out to be my weirdest night ever.

• • •

We commando-crawled through the long wet grass of an abandoned lot. I had the steak sandwiches in one hand and Lamb, Rosemary and Garlic pies in my pockets. I really hoped we wouldn't stumble across any hungry dogs.

Grandpa led the way, guided by a flashing red dot on his mobile phone. He said he had an app that could locate the signal from the homing gristle. I didn't ask which app. Dad would have probably asked for the name of the app.

Caarkula's lair was at the back of the block. At least we assumed it was.

'I'm getting a really strong signal now,'

Grandpa said. In front of us was a faded pink and white Mr Whippy van. Above the grimy service window were two oversized plastic ice-creams, bent and draped in cobwebs. The tyres were flat.

'Shhhhhh,' said the Grand Saucerer, with finger to lips.

'Shhhhhh,' said Saucerer Ameet to me.

'Pete, have you got the steak sandwiches?' Grandpa whispered.

I held up the paper bag with the sandwiches.

'Saucerer Ameet, have you got the sausage on a stick?' Grandpa whispered.

Ameet opened his jacket like a spy. His eyes gleamed in the moonlight. 'One sausage on a stick.'

Grandpa gritted his teeth. 'Okay. Let's do it.'

We stalked the van like hunters approaching a deer. Grandpa pulled the door on the driver's side. It opened with a horrible metallic screech. In a flash, Grandpa had one of his safety pies out of his pocket, brandishing it like a shield.

But nothing moved.

We breathed again. Grandpa re-pocketed the pie.

We entered the van. It smelled dusty and abandoned. There were cobwebs all over the old ice-cream fridges. In one corner was a pile of pie

scraps—pastry, cellophane, congealed meat. It was a serious stash.

One of those pie skeletons is mine, I thought.

'There,' mouthed the Grand Saucerer, pointing at something white and yellow in the corner. It was a strange misshapen rectangle, about the size of a large shoebox, but bumpy all over, like pineapple skin. It had a lid of sorts, and was wider at one end than the other.

My heart skipped a beat. It was a coffin. Caarkula's coffin.

We crept closer.

I could see the coffin more clearly now. Surely it wasn't . . . urgh, yuck! The coffin was made out of old chips, all mashed together.

Grandpa edged closer and stooped down towards the chip coffin.

'Steak sandwich,' he whispered to me, holding out one hand. I handed him the bag. He pulled out the cold steak sandwich.

'Sausage on a stick,' he said to Saucerer Ameet.

'Sausage on a stick,' Saucerer Ameet whispered to the Grand Saucerer, like he was a nurse assisting in an operation.

Then I noticed Grandpa had a small mallet. A bit like the one Dad takes to hammer in pegs when we go camping.

'Grandpa, what are you doing?' I whispered.

'It's the only way to kill a vampie seagull,' Grandpa said. 'You have to drive a steak sandwich through its heart.'

'With a sausage on a stick?' I said.

'Exactly,' Grandpa murmured. 'With a sausage on a stick.'

Grandpa was lowering his left hand towards the chip coffin. He wasn't going to actually touch those old chips with his bare hands, was he? He absolutely was. Grandpa inched open the lid. I wanted to run. We were at the back of an abandoned lot in a broken down Mr Whippy van confronting the most notorious vampie seagull of the age.

Grandpa lifted the lid some more . . .

There was Caarkula, on his back. He eyes were closed. The little black cape was tied at the neck. His orange vampie tooth gleamed at the front of his sharp beak. I strained to see if he was moving but Caarkula's seagull breast was completely motionless.

Grandpa placed the steak sandwich across Caarkula's chest. Then he gestured to Ameet for the sausage on a stick. He held the sausage on a stick in his left hand, and the mallet in his right. He wound up to strike.

'Grandpa,' I said, suddenly desperate. 'You can't kill it. It's a living thing!

'It's not living. It's undead,' said Grandpa.

'It's a seagull!' I exclaimed.

'No, it's a vampie seagull,' he replied. 'It's Caarkula.'

Maybe it was the sound of his name, maybe it was the smell of the take-away food, maybe he sensed his imminent death. Caarkula's double-lidded eyes flipped open and, with a terrible screeching, he flapped his great wings.

'Crrrrrrr! Caaaaark!'

'Safety pies!' Ameet screamed.

I fumbled in my jacket pocket for a cold Lamb, Rosemary and Garlic pie. Grandpa held his pie way out in front, eyes blazing, backing away from Caarkula like a matador eyeing a wounded bull.

'Crrrrrrr! Caaaaaaaark!'

Caarkula flew at us.

All I could see was the wide open beak and the black vampie eye. Grandpa ducked. I dived. Ameet threw his safety pie. He was an expert aim. When I looked up, the pie had been speared by Caarkula's orange beak. The garlic did the trick. The horrible beast spat and spluttered and then retreated out of the van and into the night.

There was a long silence.

'I'm sorry, Grandpa,' I said, feeling the sting of tears. 'I woke him up.'

Grandpa shrugged. 'It's not your fault, Pete. Everyone freaks out on their first mission.'

'But we could have got him? We could have finished Caarkula for good.'

'Maybe, maybe not.' Grandpa began to stomp on Caarkula's chip coffin, turning it into a gluggy, potatoey mess. 'Well, we destroyed this lair, anyway. The night's certainly not wasted.' He rubbed my neck. 'And I got to do it with my new Saucerer's Apprentice.'

'Will we ever catch him?' I said.

'Of course we will!' the Grand Saucerer said.

Saucerer Ameet punched the air with the sausage on a stick and said, 'Yeaaaah!'

We took the long route home. At the 7-Eleven, we farewelled Ameet and fed our safety pies to a stray dog. Then we wandered back to the car.

'How will we catch him, Grandpa?'

'We will be vigilant,' Grandpa said. 'At the football, we will strive for perfect pies. If we achieve perfect pies, Caarkula won't be far behind.'

'What if we don't get another perfect pie for years?'

Grandpa squeezed my hand and gazed into the starry night. He had a faraway look about him. I thought I heard a distant 'caaark' high up in the rustling trees. We were at the car now. The adventure was over. The Grand Saucerer unlocked the car and gave his apprentice's hand a final squeeze.

'We just keep on eating pies, Pete. We keep on eating pies.'

MOMO AND ME

by

Sally Rippin

Some kids have pet goldfish. Others have dogs or cats. We have Momo.

Momo is a monkey. Dad is a scientist at a very experimental laboratory. He believes monkeys and kids are pretty much the same. One day he brought Momo home to live with us. We are not allowed to call him our pet. We are meant to think of him as our little brother. Our very mischievous little brother.

Momo's favourite food is spaghetti. Most monkeys like bananas, but Momo loves spaghetti. Especially with lots of cheese on top. He likes to wind it round his fork, round his fingers, round his nose, round his tail, around his whole hairy monkey body until Mum says, 'Oh, my Lordy Lord. That monkey will be the death of me.'

Then Dad says, 'Don't talk about our son like that!' and Mum gives him one of her looks. Mum thinks three noisy children is more than enough for

her to cope with without a monkey child, too. She says, 'One more naughty move from that monkey and it's back to where he came from!' That's usually when we take Momo out the back to play on the jungle gym. Of all my siblings, Momo is easily the best on the jungle gym.

Dad says we are lucky to have Momo as a little brother. When he was growing up he only had his big bossy sister, Thelma, to play with. Thelma is nothing like Dad. Sometimes Dad likes to joke that Momo is more like us than he is like his sister. But Thelma is his only sister and she doesn't have any other family so every Sunday she comes for lunch at our place.

Aunt Thelma likes to think of herself as 'artistic'. She says Dad got the science brain but she is the artist of the family. We have lots of things at our place that Aunt Thelma has made for us: ornaments, cups and lots of paintings of her dog. Every Sunday morning, before Aunt Thelma comes over, Mum brings them all out of their hiding place at the back of the cupboard and displays them around the house. Then, every Sunday evening she packs them all away again. I don't think Mum is a big fan of Aunt Thelma's artwork.

Aunt Thelma especially likes to make her own hats. Aunt Thelma says you can tell a lot about a person by the kind of hat they wear. This is most certainly true. Aunt Thelma is the only person I know to ever wear a hat indoors. Especially a big brightly-coloured handmade hat. This really does tell you a lot about Aunt Thelma.

One Sunday Aunt Thelma arrived at our house wearing a particularly elaborate hat. It had a big bird's nest perched on top of it with a small bird sitting in it. The bird was painted blue and made of clay. When you looked at it straight on, one of its eyes looked up at the ceiling and the other out the door. It was the craziest looking hat I had ever seen. Momo must have thought so, too, because he jumped up and down excitedly when Aunt Thelma walked in the door, hooting and screeching.

'Well, I'm very happy to see you, too, Momo,' Aunt Thelma said, smiling stiffly, even though I knew she wasn't.

'Oh, Thelma, what a marvellous hat!' Mum said as Aunt Thelma walked into the room. 'You have really outdone yourself this time!'

But even Mum, who is so polite with everyone, found it hard to keep her mouth from quivering.

Imagine someone walking into your house with a bird's nest on their head. It's not something that happens every day.

'Why, thank you, dear!' Aunt Thelma said, admiring herself in the mirror above the fireplace. 'I have noticed more people than usual looking my way since I've been wearing it.'

Aunt Thelma was so proud of her fancy hat that she kept it on all afternoon. She kept it on in the kitchen. She kept it on the lounge room. She even kept it on when she went to the—Oh, well, you don't need to know about that. What you do need to know is that, most importantly, Aunt Thelma kept her hat on when we all sat down to lunch. Most people don't wear hats when they sit down at the table, but that's Aunt Thelma for you.

I sat across from Aunt Thelma and, as always, Momo sat next to me because I am the best at keeping him out of trouble. Momo has quite good manners for a monkey, but he can get a little distracted. He doesn't mean to be naughty, but sometimes he just can't help himself. He gets curious about things and, I tell you now, when this happens, there's almost nothing we can do about it. This is when Momo is definitely more monkey than little brother.

As I poured myself a glass of water, I noticed out of the corner of my eye that Momo's fingers had begun to twitch. He was staring very intently at Aunt Thelma's hat. Or, more precisely, the bluebird in the nest on Aunt Thelma's hat. He had been watching that bluebird all day. This got me worried. Very worried. 'Sit nicely, Momo,' I whispered as he started to fidget on his seat. 'Lunch will be here soon. Dad's making spaghetti. You like spaghetti, don't you?' I signed the words 'lunch' and 'spaghetti' with my hands.

Momo looked up at me with his big brown eyes and nodded excitedly. He signed 'spaghetti' with his hands, then rubbed his tummy.

'Oh, look, he's hungry,' my little brother Sammy said. 'You hungry, Momo?' he asked and made the sign for 'hungry'.

Momo nodded again. Then, before I could stop him, he hopped up from the seat beside me and sat down across the table, next to Aunt Thelma to peer more closely at her hat.

Aunt Thelma hadn't noticed Momo sit down beside her. She was much too busy telling Mum all about a new painting she was working on. Mum was nodding politely, trying to look interested,

as she darted in and out of the kitchen fetching the plates and cutlery to set the table. Dad had already excused himself to put the pasta on. It was up to me to watch Momo.

Momo's eyes grew wide and his fingers twitched again. I knew this meant trouble. Big trouble. And I was in charge of Momo at the dinner table. So big trouble for Momo meant big trouble for me, too.

'Momo, come and sit on my lap,' I called, smiling sweetly. I patted my lap.

Momo shook his head from side to side.

'Come on, Momo,' my big brother Pete said. 'Go and sit on Violet's lap. She wants to give you a cuddle. Don't you, Violet?'

I nodded and patted my lap again. Once again, Momo shook his head slowly.

I stood up to walk towards Momo, but within two seconds flat, he had climbed up the back of Aunt Thelma's chair and snatched off her hat. Then he darted out of the dining room and was gone.

'My hat!' shrieked Aunt Thelma. 'My hat! That rotten monkey has stolen my hat!'

'Momo!' I shouted chasing after him. Sammy and Pete both chased after me.

'Oh my Lordy Lord! That monkey will be the death of me!' Mum gasped as we stumbled past her.

'It's okay, Aunt Thelma,' I yelled. 'We'll get your hat back!'

We ran down the hallway, but Momo had locked himself in the bathroom. Pete banged on the door. 'Momo! Open the door this minute,' he shouted. 'Give us back Aunt Thelma's hat.'

There was no reply. Dad appeared in the hallway with a pair of tongs in his hand. 'What's going on?' he asked.

'It's Momo!' Sammy cried. 'He's stolen Aunt Thelma's hat.'

'And now he's locked himself in the bathroom,' said Pete.

Dad bit down hard on his lip. We could tell he was trying not to laugh. 'The bird's nest hat?' he snorted.

'Dad!' I said. 'It's not funny. You know what Mum said. One more naughty thing and you'll have to take Momo back to where he came from!'

'Your mum would never do that to your little brother,' Dad said, frowning.

'Dad!' all three of us said together.

'Okay, okay,' Dad said. 'Look, you talk Momo out

of the bathroom and I'll go and calm Thelma down. It will all be okay, all right?'

Dad rushed back into the dining room to where Aunt Thelma was wailing.

'Momo,' I called. But there was no answer. 'Momo,' I called again.

We all put our ears to the door to hear what Momo was doing. A strange noise came from the other side.

'Is that *chewing*?' Pete asked. 'Is Momo *eating* something?'

We listened carefully. It certainly sounded like there was some crunching going on.

'Oh no! He's not eating Aunt Thelma's hat, is he?' Sammy said.

'Why would he eat her hat?' said Pete.

Sammy and Pete looked at each other and giggled.

'It's not funny!' I said, frowning. 'He could really be in trouble this time.'

I put my mouth to the door and called out gently, 'Momo, Momo. Come on, Momo. If you come out I'll let you play with my Barbie campervan.'

We waited and waited. Finally Momo opened the door. His arms were behind his back and he had a long yellow string hanging from his mouth. He

didn't look very happy. In fact, he didn't look happy at all.

'Momo,' Pete said angrily. 'Where's Aunt Thelma's hat? You didn't eat it, did you?'

Momo shook his head. Then brought his hands around from behind his back. In one hand he had Aunt Thelma's hat. In his other hand he had Aunt Thelma's kooky clay bird. Then, he wrinkled up his nose, coughed and spluttered, and spat out a small piece of yellow string.

'The bird's nest,' Sammy gasped. 'From Aunt Thelma's hat. Momo ate the bird's nest!'

'Why would Momo eat the nest?' Pete asked. 'It's made from string.'

Just then, I knew what had happened. The nest may have only been string but curled around the sitting bird it had looked just like Momo's favourite food. 'Spaghetti!' I said. 'Momo thought it was spaghetti.'

'Momo! Cough it up!' Pete said. But it was too late. Momo had swallowed the whole bird's nest except for that tiny piece of string.

Sammy snorted with laughter.

'Sammy,' I snapped. 'This is not funny.'

Dad appeared in the hallway again, looking

worried. 'Oh, thank goodness,' he said when he saw Momo. 'How's the hat?'

We were all silent. Momo hung his head.

'Oh no,' said Dad. 'It's bad, isn't it?'

Pete nodded.

'How bad?'

Pete shook his head. He held out the parts of Aunt Thelma's hat. The hat was okay. Even the bird was okay. But the nest was gone. It had vanished into Momo's tummy.

Now we were all worried. If Aunt Thelma didn't get her hat back in one piece this would be trouble with a capital 'T'. We felt sure Mum would make Dad send Momo away now.

'What are we going to do?' Sammy said. His bottom lip quivered.

'Don't worry, Sammy,' I said. 'Dad will figure something out.'

Dad frowned. 'We'll just have to make another nest,' he said. 'Surely, it can't be that hard. Have we got any string in the art cupboard, Violet?'

I shook my head. 'I used it all up for my project last weekend.'

Dad checked the drawers in the hallway cupboard where Mum kept all her sewing stuff. There were pins and needles and even an old sock puppet, but no string.

Momo started to whimper. I picked him up and cuddled him. 'It's okay, Momo,' I said. 'We'll think of something.' Just then I had an idea. 'I know. Have you served up the spaghetti yet, Dad?'

'No,' said Dad. And he seemed to know exactly where I was heading. 'Oh good thinking, my girl,' he grinned.

'Come on, Momo,' I said. 'We can fix this.' I swung

him up into my arms and we all dashed off into the kitchen. Dad grabbed a handful of spaghetti out of the colander and rolled it into a ball. Then he stuck it on Aunt Thelma's hat with a few pins. On top of the spaghetti nest he stuck the funny clay bird. It looked almost exactly like before. No wonder Momo had got it mixed up with our lunch!

'Perfect,' said Dad, and Momo grinned happily.

'Do you think she'll be able to tell the difference?' I said.

'Nah,' said Dad. 'Her eyesight is terrible. How else could she have created such a hideous hat?'

'Dad!' I said, giggling, and we all ran into the dining room.

'Oh, my hat,' Aunt Thelma said, almost hyperventilating. 'I hope that dreadful monkey hasn't dirtied it?'

'His name is Momo,' Dad said. 'And, don't worry, it's still in perfect condition.' He helped her fasten it back onto her head. 'Really, Thelma, you look as splendid as ever.'

'Well, I have been told my hats are quite flattering,' she said, fluffing up her hair.

'Well, that was a close call,' Mum frowned, giving Dad a look. Dad popped Momo in his seat again,

and patted his furry head. Momo smiled up at him sweetly, just like our perfect little brother.

The rest of us sat down at the table, trying not to snigger, our hearts beating hard. We didn't dare look at each other. Even Dad didn't look us in the eye as he served out big bowls of spaghetti. But Mum glared at us, one by one, trying to work out what was so funny. When Momo pushed back his bowl of spaghetti she narrowed her eyes. 'Hmmm. That's strange,' she said. 'Momo usually loves spaghetti. I wonder what's got into him?'

Sammy giggled and Pete and I snorted. Mum's eyes widened as they went from Momo's bowl to Aunt Thelma's hat. She put her hand over her mouth.

'Oh my Lordy Lord,' she gasped. 'Aunt Thelma. Your hat.'

We all held our breath. Even Momo stopped breathing for a moment.

'Yes?' Aunt Thelma said, looking up from her bowl of spaghetti. 'You were commenting on my hat?'

Mum took a deep breath. 'It's just splendid, Aunt Thelma,' she said, trying not to laugh. 'Really, I have to say, this would have to be your best hat yet. You've really and truly outdone yourself this time.'

'Why, thank you, dear!' Aunt Thelma said, smiling and nodding. And as she nodded we watched the tiniest blob of Bolognese sauce slide slowly down her neck.

THE QUIBBLES

by

Jaclyn Moriarty

You will know who I am.

Everybody does.

Barnabas Theodore Jarmuschian the Third, King of the Realms of Dartmeter, Emperor of the Islets from Hither to Thither, Lord of all the Surrounding Bits and Bobs Including Any Treasure or Chip Packets that Might Blow onto the Beach.

Most people just call me Barney.

The day I want to tell you about happened last year. Back then, I was taking a break from my Kingdom. I was living in a flat on Phillip Street, Neutral Bay. Across the road from the bus stop, around the corner from My Little Cupcake. Perfect.

Next door to me lived Callie-Rose and her two children. Tim was ten and Emily was six.

Every time I saw her, Callie-Rose yawned. 'Sorry, Barney!' she said, smiling around the yawn.

'Bit sleepy!' And no wonder. Seven days a week, she worked. Yet still they never had enough money! Tim's toes poked out of his sneakers! Emily's jeans were as frayed as cobwebs! Friends would come to play and I'd hear them shout: 'Where's your Xbox? Where's your Lego? Where's your Rainbow Mermaid Barbie?' And then: 'WHAT? YOU DON'T? HOW CAN YOU NOT?!'

Some nights I heard Callie-Rose crying.

• • •

A large woman named Patty took care of the children while their mother worked. Patty's cheeks were as pink as frosted cupcakes. Whenever I saw her, I said, 'Great idea! A cupcake! Let's go get one!' And she would blink in confusion.

One Saturday, I walked out of my flat and there was Patty, knocking on Callie-Rose's door. The door opened.

'I can't take the kids today,' Patty said.

'Oh dear,' said Callie-Rose. 'It's their activities today!'

'Skip them,' Patty advised.

Callie-Rose bit her lip. 'It's their only treat.

My Aunt Hilda pays for them because she thinks they build character.'

'If your Aunt Hilda had any character of her own,' Patty said, 'she'd help out with their food and clothes too.'

'You can't take them for just *half* their activities?' Callie-Rose tried.

'Sorry.' Patty shrugged. 'I've got a rotten cold.' She coughed like a bulldozer to prove it.

'Poor thing,' Callie-Rose said. 'Go home and rest. The kids will just have to watch telly while I work.'

Here I straightened my royal shoulders and marched over. 'No, they will not!' I said. 'For I will look after them today!'

And that is how I came to take Tim and Emily to their activities.

• • •

I wore my best suit and tie.

We packed the children's gear into my duffel bag. That was when I felt the first quibble.

It was in my right shoe.

I ignored it and we set out.

• • •

The first activity of the day was Swimming.

Tim's class was at one end of the pool, and Emily's was at the other. So I strode up and down the pool between them. Sometimes I bumped into Tim's teacher, a girl named Monica. She was also striding up and down the pool, calling instructions to her class.

Each time I bumped into Monica, she said, 'Whoops!' and I replied, 'I forgive you.'

But after the fifth time, I'd had enough.

'Excuse me,' I said. 'It's only a little thing. But the children are in the water. Yet you are out here!'

Monica grinned. 'This is how we do it with Dolphins,' she said.

Dolphins? Dolphins?

I let it go.

I pointed down the pool at Emily's class. 'That teacher is in the pool. Learn from him! Get into the pool! As a bonus, you'll stop bumping into me.'

By now Tim's class had stopped swimming. They were bobbing about in the water, watching us.

'But those are Jellyfish,' Monica replied.

I could no longer let it go.

‘Look at them, Monica!’ I waved at the pool. ‘They have arms! Legs! Noses! Tim, show the teacher your nose!’

Tim pulled off his goggles.

‘You see!’ I said. ‘Not dolphins! Not jellyfish! But children! These are children!’

Monica laughed nervously. Poor thing. All this time she’d been thinking she was teaching dolphins.

‘Into the pool,’ I urged and I was about to give her a gentle push, when I noticed something amazing down the other end.

Emily’s teacher was a boy named Zac. And he was handing out little white kickboards! The children were now holding these and kicking!

‘Excuse me!’ I shouted.

Zac did not hear.

I hurried down the pool. ‘EXCUSE ME!’ Still nothing.

So I jumped into the pool.

My suit really dragged me down.

I pushed my way across to Zac. He stared, eyes wide.

‘Just a teeny thing,’ I said. ‘But you’ve given the children kickboards!’

He nodded, eyes still wide.

'You've . . . given . . . them . . . boards,' I repeated slowly.

'Yes?'

'Boards float!'

Now he squinted.

I had to spell it out. 'The children are not really swimming,' I said. 'The boards are holding them up!'

'Oh!' Zac laughed. He started talking about technique or something. I don't really know. I stopped listening. The quibble in my shoe was going mad now. Jumbling around between my toes. They get like that in water.

'Chant this to yourself before you fall asleep each night,' I told Zac hurriedly. 'Boards float! Boards float! That way you'll always remember.' I hauled myself out of the pool.

Water poured from my suit like rain.

'Oh, and you do know these are children?' I called. 'Not jellyfish? Monica didn't know!'

Zac scratched his head.

I sloshed back down the pool, sat on the edge, and wrung out my suit.

• • •

After Swimming, we walked to the next activity.

'Ouch!' I said hopping. 'Another quibble!'

'What's a quibble?' Emily asked.

Her brother answered. 'It's a small complaint or criticism.'

'Actually,' I said, 'quibbles are tiny creatures that get into your shoes. They're the size of peas. But sharp and pointy. And they drive! you! crazy!'

Here I jumped up and down.

Jumping doesn't hurt the quibbles. They just hide inside your toenails and wait until you stop.

The children also waited, but they did not hide inside my toenails. They stood and stared at me.

• • •

At Tennis, I had to stop the lesson three times.

'Just a tiny thing!' I shouted. 'But that's not how you serve!'

'Eh?' said the teacher.

I ran onto the court. I showed him the correct way. You whistle a tune before you throw the ball. I couldn't believe he didn't know that.

'Only a minor matter!' I called a bit later. 'But take down that net!'

'What?' said the teacher.

I pointed. A net ran right across the court! 'It's getting in the way! Balls keep hitting it!'

I offered to pull it down but the teacher said he'd quite like to keep it there, thanks.

'One more teensy matter!' I bellowed, when the lesson was winding up. 'But what about the dance?'

'Um?' said the teacher.

'The dance for the tennis balls?' I said. 'To thank them for letting you play tennis?'

The teacher said that what they did instead of dancing was, they collected the balls and put them in this basket. He showed me the basket.

That didn't seem the same to me at all, but right then another quibble dug into my heel so I hopped away.

• • •

At Karate, they had left hook and right jab mixed up.

And they thought you were supposed to hold your fists up to protect your chin! You never protect your chin! You hold your fists above your head and protect your crown!

Of course, the children weren't wearing crowns, but everyone should plan on becoming a king or queen one day.

I called all this from the wall, and the teachers ignored me. But when the children paired up and started 'sparring'— pretending to hit and kick each other—I rushed right in among them.

'Run away!' I cried. 'Climb out that window! Hop up onto that pile of mats!'

Many of the children obeyed me, and now the teachers shouted and chased them, and bellowed at me to shut my trap, and everything fell apart.

It was so lucky I was there that day.

• • •

The final activity was Guitar.

We set out across the park. The children were quiet. They swapped their guitars from one shoulder to the other.

'One moment,' I said.

I sat down on the grass and pulled off my shoes. There were now eight quibbles in each. I thumped the shoes hard on the grass. There went the quibbles dashing away! I lunged after them, slapping my hands here! there! here! But of course I missed.

'Nobody can ever catch quibbles,' I said to Emily. 'I don't know why I bother trying.'

'Why do you want to catch them?'

'Tipping them out isn't enough,' I explained, 'they just rush back into your shoes first chance they get.'

'It must be awful,' Emily said, 'having quibbles.'

Tim made a noise like *tch*. 'He doesn't have

quibbles in his shoes,' he said. 'He has pebbles or gravel or something.'

He strode off. He seemed really fed up.

I didn't blame him. All day long his teachers made mistakes!

I tied my laces and followed.

• • •

At Guitar, a group of children sat in a circle, guitars on their knees.

'You can wait outside,' Tim suggested.

'But I see a spare chair next to you!'

I sat on it. The teacher, Mr Bank, blinked at me. He was a thin fellow in shorts.

'E minor, C major, D minor, A major!' he barked suddenly. I gasped in fright. Slowly, the children began to strum.

'Stop!' Mr Bank boomed. 'You offend me!' He put his hands over his ears. 'You!' he shouted at Emily. 'D minor!'

Emily blinked. Her fingers trembled. She played. It sounded wrong. She tried again.

Mr Bank sighed. 'What did I do to deserve this?' he muttered.

Emily frowned to herself. 'Oh!' she said. 'I remember now!' She pressed her fingers to different strings but Mr Bank held up his hand. 'You have assaulted my ears enough.'

A pale pink washed across Emily's face.

The lesson continued. Mr Bank taught the children chords and scales. He shouted at a boy for playing too fast. He moaned at a girl who was 'boring him into a coma' by playing too slowly.

'Now we learn a new song,' he said. 'This is—'

'Excuse me,' I said.

Mr Bank raised an eyebrow.

'Here we go,' Tim sighed.

'Just a small thing,' I said. 'But in the Realms of Dartmeter, the guitar is a sacred instrument.'

Tim covered his face with his hands.

'Not just guitar,' I added. 'All instruments. Music is beautiful, you see, and must always be taught beautifully.'

Tim tilted his head slightly.

'When you shout and boom, roll your eyes and twist your face at children, you are being ugly. And music does not like ugliness.'

Beside me, Tim dropped his hands from his face. Emily stared.

'Come to think of it,' I said, 'that's not a small thing, it's huge! Come, Tim! Emily! Let's find you a new teacher!'

And I threw back my chair.

As we left the room, I got a glimpse of Mr Bank's face. Exactly like a teapot with its lid wide open.

• • •

Outside, we walked back across the park.

I stopped at the swing and emptied my shoes. I grabbed at the quibbles but, of course, they swerved and crept back in.

I stopped at a seesaw and tried again. Same thing.

Tim and Emily watched me.

'These quibbles of yours,' Tim said eventually. 'What do they look like?'

'There goes one!' I said.

Tim and Emily frowned down at the grass. A spark of crimson zipped by Tim's foot.

'I saw it!' Emily said.

Tim was quiet. 'Me too,' he said.

He and Emily stepped away. They whispered. They turned back to me.

'Can we help you catch them?'

'You won't be able to,' I said. 'But you can try!'

They whispered again, then tipped their things out of my duffel bag.

'When we say now,' Tim said, 'hold your shoes high in the air and give them a good shake.'

'And when we say guitar, lift it up,' Emily added.

I waited, my shoes ready.

'Now!' they cried.

What happened next was astonishing.

I shook the shoes and here came the quibbles rushing into the air! A swarm of crimson beads!

Emily, tennis racquets in both hands, thwacked them!

Tim threw a right jab, a left hook, and thwacked them back!

Tennis racquets swung! Hands swiped the air!

The children moved closer together, surrounding the quibbles! Herding them into a tighter and tighter circle!

'Guitar!' they shouted.

I held it high.

Thwack, swipe, thwack, swipe, and the quibbles went rolling into the guitar!

'Towel!' Tim said and, like a flash, Emily slid her damp pool towel over the guitar's opening. She wrapped it around the guitar, and tied it tight.

I blinked.

Then I burst into laughter.

In all my days, I had never seen a single quibble caught and here the children had captured at least fifteen.

• • •

We had cupcakes to celebrate.

The quibbles rattled around in Emily's guitar. 'How will I play that now?' she wondered.

'Simple,' I said. 'You won't. I'll buy you a new guitar.'

We stopped in the music shop and did just that, and then I took the children to their flat. As it happened, that was the last time I saw them, for that very night I was called home on urgent business.

Yesterday, I sent them a postcard.

Dear Tim and Emily,

Rainy weather here but I am cosy in my palace. I've been very busy avoiding war with Cut-Throat Isle (lucky), but I did find time to sell the quibbles. A professor who teaches quibble theory at the university was VERY excited to get a guitar full of them. (Don't worry, they are well-fed and very comfortable.) I got a fair price and have just deposited it in your mother's account. It comes to around 12 million Australian dollars. I do hope Patty's cold is better.

Kind regards,
Barney

PS We now have activities every Saturday at the palace! You must come visit. You will find our teachers are rather better than yours.

CORN CHIP BELIEBER

by

Meg McKinlay

I'm eating lunch on the school oval when I find Justin Bieber in my lunchbox.

To be fair, it's my friend Max who spots him first.

At the time, I'm a bit distracted. Steven Seagull, the legendary lunchtime bandit, is giving me the side-eye. I'm pretty sure he's getting ready to swoop in and steal my corn chips.

That's where Justin Bieber is—in the corn chips.

One particular corn chip.

The one that's in my hand, heading right for my mouth.

I'm about to bite down on it when Max yells, 'Zack!'

At first I think he's trying to warn me about Steven Seagull. I don't know why though, because everyone knows about Steven. The first thing you learn when you start at Westwood Primary isn't how to write your name or tie your shoelaces. It's how to stop Steven Seagull stealing your lunch.

Steven Seagull doesn't muck around. He doesn't bother with that lame, 'Feed me! I only have one leg!' routine some seagulls try. He just fixes you with his steely gaze and dive bombs your Vegemite sandwich.

'Don't worry!' I say. 'I see him.'

But Max yanks my hand away from my mouth. 'Is it just me or does that corn chip look exactly like Justin Bieber?'

I don't see it at first. I mean—how can it be Justin Bieber? It's a corn chip.

But then Max gets me to hold it a bit further from my face. He angles my arm to the left.

'See?'

And now I do. It's all there in the little black spots—his Bieber cheeks, his nose, his puppy-dog eyes. There's even a funny sort of ripple that looks exactly like his hair.

'Wow,' I say. 'Cannot be unseen. Here.' I hand the chip to Max. There's no way I can eat it now. 'They should put a warning on these. *May contain traces of Bieber*.'

Liza Morellini turns around. She's sitting behind Max with Kayley Collins and Evie Chung. 'Hey, how come you guys are talking about Justin Bieber?'

I feel my cheeks flush. 'We're not. We—'

'Yes you are.' Kayley nods. 'I heard you say his name.'

'We have Bieber radar,' Evie says. 'It's a thing.' She points at their lunchboxes. Liza's has 'Future Mrs Bieber' written on it in texta, and Kayley's has a 'Bieber Fever' sticker plastered along one side. Evie's has a heart-shaped keychain hanging off it that says, 'I'm a Belieber'.

'Wait,' Liza says. 'Is he touring?'

Kayley's eyes widen. 'Is he coming here?'

'He can't be,' Evie says. 'I would have heard about it. I follow him on Facebook, Twitter, Instagram and Tumblr. This one time, he even—'

'Liked your status!' Kaylie and Liza chorus, rolling their eyes. 'We know, Evie!'

Evie's face goes red. 'I'm just saying. If he was coming, I'd know.'

A slow smile creeps across Max's face. 'Oh, he's coming. In fact he's here right now.'

He holds up Corn Chip Bieber. He holds it at the right distance, on the right angle.

Evie squints, frowning, but Liza squeals. 'OMG! It looks exactly like him!'

I spot the exact moment Evie sees it because every part of her face changes. It's like the sun's come out from behind a cloud. 'It's him! I can't believe it. It's actually JUSTIN BIEBER.'

At the sound of her voice, heads turn across the oval. It's like that moment in a zombie movie when the undead get a whiff of human flesh and start lumbering towards the smell.

In no time at all, we're surrounded by kids.

The girls are flipping their hair as if Corn Chip Bieber is the real deal. As if he's about to pick up a microphone and pluck them out of the crowd to dance on stage.

The boys are sticking their fingers in their mouths and pretending to be sick.

But they all have something in common. They all want to get a closer look at Corn Chip Bieber.

And that's when I get an idea.

I take the chip from Max and slip it carefully inside my lunchbox, then snap the lid shut.

'I'm sorry,' I say. 'Justin Bieber is only doing limited appearances today.'

Max gives me a weird look. 'Zack, what are you—?'

'Come on.' I grab his arm. 'I'll explain in a minute.'

As we push through the crowd, for just a second I imagine myself in a dark suit and sunglasses, whisking Bieber away from a crush of fans.

If this was real-life Bieber, we'd be escorting him in a glass elevator up to some fancy hotel suite.

But this is Corn Chip Bieber, and that means we're going to the library—a place neither of us has ever been seen at lunchtime—because we've got some googling to do.

• • •

By the next morning, we have everything organised.

Max has made up some flyers and I've borrowed a fancy jewellery box from Mum. Corn Chip Bieber is reclining inside on some shiny silver padding.

I told Mum the box was for a school project. I wasn't exactly lying.

It's a project to make as much money as we can, and we're doing it at school.

Yesterday's library time was brilliant.

This is a sentence I never thought I'd say, but it's true. On the library computers, we quickly learned two key facts:

i) People have been finding weird faces in food since food and faces were invented. Mostly, they're faces of Jesus and the Virgin Mary. We didn't come across a single Bieber food face.

ii) People will pay a lot of money for anything Bieber-related. This includes sweaty towels, strands of hair, and air he might possibly once have breathed.

These two facts have two things in common:

i) They are extremely weird.
ii) They are very good news for us.

We pass the flyers around at recess and word spreads fast.

Corn Chip Bieber is cheap at the price: $2 each for a private viewing or 50c per person for a group of five.

If you're really keen, you can buy the True Belieber VIP Experience: $4 to hold the box yourself; includes one photo.

I wasn't sure about photos at first. If people could see it that way, why would they pay us for a look?

But Max made a solid point. It was free advertising, he said. And a photo wasn't the same as seeing Bieber in the flesh.

Or in the corn.

If you want a photo, you run the risk of having your phone confiscated by teachers on yard duty, but that's not our problem.

'All care and no responsibility,' says Max. I'm not sure what he means by that but the True Beliebers nod gravely and fork over the money.

And that's what really matters.

It's nearly all profit. Our only expense is the $2 we slip some kid in Year 3 to warn us when a teacher's coming. When he whistles, we hide the price list and the cash tin. We pretend we're just doing community service—sharing our Bieber with others out of the goodness of our hearts.

Teachers love community service. They love goodness. And hearts.

• • •

By lunchtime, we're rolling in money.

By halfway through lunchtime, we could probably shower in it. There's a line of kids stretching halfway across the oval.

That's when we shut up shop.

'Corn Chip Bieber needs his beauty sleep,' I say. 'He's doing back-to-back shows.'

The crowd is not happy.

'You can't do that!' they say.

'But I was next!'

'I've been waiting for ages!'

'So come back tomorrow.' Max and I smile as we walk away. When you tell people they can't have something, it makes them want it even more.

• • •

For the next few days, business is crazy.

Kids can't get enough of the Bieb. Some come back for a second look. Then a third.

On Thursday, we add a new item to our product list: Selfie with Corn Chip Bieber. It's a bargain at just $4.50.

It's also very cunning. It means kids who've already coughed up $4 for a photo come back and pay again. Because who wants a photo of a Justin Bieber corn chip when you can have one of yourself posing next to it?

'Max,' I say. 'You're a sales genius.'

'I know,' he replies. 'I reckon I've found my future career.'

I slap him on the back. I'm not sure how many openings there are for food-face entrepreneurs, but I guess everyone has to have a dream.

A few kids try to cash in on our success. Jeremy Collins and Morgan Jakovich buy up packets of chips from the canteen and search them all, trying to find one that looks like someone famous.

At one point, Jeremy yells, 'Look! It's Harry Styles!' and a bunch of Directioners sprint across

the oval. But when they realise it's just a Pringle with texta on it, they come charging back.

A couple of kids declare themselves to be Bieber-intolerant. The canteen lady puts up a sign declaring all snack foods to be guaranteed 100% Bieber-free.

Evie hangs around the line trying to get kids to pay 50c—and then 20c and then 10c—for a look at her screenshot. 'Justin Bieber liked my status,' she says. 'See?'

Rachel Tan rolls her eyes. 'You realise it isn't actually Justin Bieber, right? As if he does his own Facebook.'

Evie flushes. She tosses her hair and points at our jewellery box. 'Well that isn't him either. It's a CORN CHIP!'

'I know that,' says Rachel. 'It's not the same.' Then she hands over $4.50 and starts practising her poses.

• • •

At recess on Friday, Max is handing out change and I'm wrangling the line. In between, we swap ideas about what to do with our cash.

As of now, we've got $127.50, which is enough for two season passes to Water World (my idea), or

ten Cheap Tuesday tickets to see the new Star Wars movie over and over and over (Max's idea).

I'm trying to convince Max how dumb his idea is without actually using the word 'dumb' when I realise I don't need to.

I point at the crowd of kids. 'We can have both. We can make another hundred bucks, easy.'

'Maybe more.' Max looks thoughtful. 'How long do you reckon the Bieb will last? Before he goes mouldy or whatever.'

'We should google it,' I say. 'Search terms might be tricky, though.'

Max grins. 'How about, "Taking care of your Corn Chip Bieber"?'

'Yeah. Or, "Top ten hacks for Bieber storage".'

He snickers. 'You won't believe how long this corn chip lasted!'

'Bieber problems? Check out this one weird trick!'

We're so busy cracking ourselves up that at first we don't see the commotion on the other side of the oval, near the road. Some cars have pulled up and people are running towards us with cameras and microphones.

As they get closer, I see they have logos on their equipment. They're news crews. From Channel Six and Channel Three and some other place I've never heard of.

When they get even closer, they start calling out.

'Boys! Where did you find the corn chip?'

'What flavour is it?'

'How much money have you made?'

Evie sidles up to me, grinning. 'I posted my selfie

on Facebook and tagged Justin. He hasn't liked it yet but I got 85 shares.'

'Oh, no.'

'Oh, yes.' Max smiles. 'More exposure, mate. All good for business.'

'Yeah, except that if a teacher finds out, our business is over. And they'll probably make us give all the money back.' I glance up towards the classrooms. Mr Emerson has finished his lap of the undercover area and is heading towards us.

'Solid point,' Max replies. 'Umm . . . '

Suddenly there's a microphone in my face. Then another.

'What a pair of entrepreneurs!'

'How's business?'

'Can we get a shot of the Bieber?'

I open my mouth and then close it again. And while I'm trying to think of what I can say that won't drop us into a steaming pile of trouble, the woman from Channel Six asks a question that stops me in my tracks.

'Will you be auctioning it on eBay?'

I shoot Max a look.

He slaps his forehead. Of course. Why didn't we think of this before?

Channel Six woman consults a small notepad. 'Did you know that an American casino paid $28,000 for a sandwich with the Virgin Mary's face on it?'

'$28,000?' All of a sudden I've got goosebumps.

Her camera guy nods. 'I remember that. It was a toasted sandwich. Ten years old.'

'Ten years old?'

Max grabs my arm. 'Mate, our Bieber is fresh.'

I feel weak at the knees. Is Bieber worth more than the Virgin Mary? I don't think I want to know the answer to that question.

'Will it be going on eBay?' the woman asks again. She reaches toward the box.

'Yes!' I grab the box and hold it high, out of reach. Suddenly, keeping Corn Chip Bieber safe is the most important thing in the world.

'$28,000,' Max whispers.

'Holy—', I reply.

And that's when Steven swoops.

He drops out of the clear blue sky and snatches Bieber, then takes off across the heads of the crowd.

I drop the box and follow.

This would usually be a waste of time because Steven is fast and clever. When he steals something, he takes it well out of reach. He sits

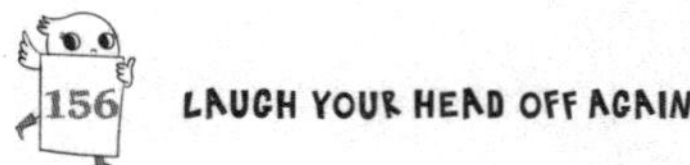

on a branch high above your head, smirking. And snacking.

He's trying to do that now. He's heading for the big gumtree, aiming for his usual spot. Only he's struggling. He's beyond arm's reach but only just. And he's slow. Slow enough that I can get close and see what's wrong.

He hasn't just got Bieber. He's taken a chunk out of the box as well. It's stuck in his beak, weighing him down. He snaps his head back and forth trying to shake it loose.

I'm directly below him when it falls. And when Bieber falls with it.

Corn Chip Bieber is plummeting towards me. I reach out my arms.

I've almost got him. *Welcome back, Bieber,* I think. *We're going to sell you on eBay for $28,000. Maybe even more.*

I can hardly wait to see how many thousands we get.

My fingertips brush the Bieber. He's within my grasp.

Then Steven dive bombs. Steven Seagull, legendary action bird, grabs Bieber with his beak.

But I've got the other end and I don't let go.

I'm tugging one way and Steven's tugging the other and then, all of a sudden, he stops. When I pull towards me, he doesn't resist. Corn Chip Bieber comes flying at me, with Steven attached. I topple backwards and then we're all on the ground together, rolling, and I'm still holding on.

'I've got him!' I yell. 'I've got Bieber.'

But there's something weird about him. He's kind of wet and mushy and . . .

'Gross,' says Kaylie. 'He's gone all soggy.'

I look up at Max. 'Do you reckon there's a market for regurgitated Bieber?'

He rolls his eyes. 'It doesn't even look like him anymore.'

Evie chokes back a sob. 'I can't believe he's dead. I need to update my status.'

At least we've still got our $127.50, I think. Maybe we can see Star Wars once and still have enough for Water World?

There's a squawking sound next to me. I turn and glare at Steven. I swear he set this whole thing up. I swear he's laughing.

'What's going on here?' Mr Emerson pushes his way through the crowd. He looks down at me. 'Why are you wrestling a defenceless bird, Zack?'

'Defenceless?' I protest. 'That's Steven Seagull! He stole my . . . ' Then I stop, because the cameras are rolling and I'm not sure I want to be on the news complaining about a corn chip.

'We do not wrestle defenceless birds at this school!' Mr Emerson thunders.

Max shakes his head. 'To be fair, I don't remember that ever being a rule.'

Mr Emerson turns on him. 'What did you—?'

Channel Six woman claps a hand over her mouth. 'Oh, that poor bird! He's injured.'

I laugh. 'Steven Seagull doesn't get injured. He . . . '

I trail off. Steven's standing all wobbly, with one leg bent up underneath him.

'Zack!' Mr Emerson hurries to Steven's side. 'What have you done?'

'That bird needs a vet,' says Channel Three guy.

'A vet? For a seagull?' Mr Emerson catches sight of the camera. He clears his throat. 'I mean to say . . . of course! Here at Westwood Primary, we are deeply concerned about animal welfare. Aren't we, boys?'

I nod, and give a weak thumbs-up. Max tries to melt back into the crowd but kids push him forward.

Mr Emerson calls for a towel and scoops

Steven up. 'This bird will receive the best possible care,' he declares loudly. Then he turns to Max and me and whispers, 'You boys will pay for this.'

And we do.

How much do we pay, you ask?

What a good question.

The vet finds nothing wrong with Steven. His leg seems fine. By the time the bell goes, he's back stalking the oval like nothing ever happened.

'He was probably just in shock,' the vet says.

But Max and I know better.

The vet takes pity on us. She gives us a lecture about the dangers of seagull wrestling, and then a 10% discount. This brings her fee to $126.

Which leaves us with enough for one-fortieth of a Water World pass, one-eighth of a movie ticket . . . or a packet of corn chips from the canteen.

As the canteen lady passes us the packet, she leans forward and whispers, 'Don't worry, boys. These are guaranteed Bieber-free.'

'Thanks,' I say.

And then we hurry to the oval, because Steven is hungry and he doesn't like to be kept waiting.

CHARLIE AND THE SILENCE OF THE LLAMAS

by

Alan Brough

'Hils?' I said. 'Do you think they'll have octopuses on this farm?'

'Negative,' said Hils.

'Good,' I said.

Hils is my best friend. We are on a bus—with the rest of my class—going to school camp. At a llama farm.

'Hils?' I said.

'Affirmative,' said Hils.

Hils says 'affirmative' instead of 'yes' (and 'negative' instead of 'no') because that is what they say in the army. Hils really, very, super wants to join the army. She acts like she is already in the army.

'You know,' I said, 'when someone has gone to the toilet and made a real stink and then they spray tons of air freshener around to cover the stink but that only makes the stink worse because now the toilet reeks of bum-stink and air-freshener-stink?'

MY CLASS	
Name of class member	**Important fact about her or him**
Simon Bolivar	Screams whenever anything happens to him. Anything.
The Lurker (Real Name: Leon Lloyd-Llewellyn)	Is dumb.
Harriet Borges	Is scared of twins.
Townes McFarlane	Wants to be a head lice breeder when he leaves school.
Krishna Malhotra	Does not believe that sparrows are actually birds. She thinks they are mice who have taught themselves to fly. I think she might be right.
Evan de la Souza	Is on a special diet where he only eats foods that will make him fart more.
Junior Silesi	Constantly stands with one of his feet on top of his other foot trying to squash his feet and make them longer. Wants to hold the record for world's biggest feet.
Rashid Naholo	Used to think he was a member of the Fijian royal family. Now is an anarchist.
Stevenson McLean	Expelled for eating dog poo. Twice.
Helna and Dayton Parish (Twins)	Went on holiday and never came back. Mrs Whyte-Wale said it was because their parents divorced. I think it is because Harriet Borges did something to them.

'Affirmative.'

'That's how this bus smells.'

'Affirmative.'

• • •

I did not want to go to school camp.

I especially did not want to go to school camp at a llama farm.

I especially did not want to go to school camp at a llama farm because I do not like animals.

You are probably thinking, 'Charlie Ian Duncan, who turns twelve next February, what is wrong with you? Everyone likes animals. Animals are cute. Animals are furry. Some animals are bacon-flavoured. How can you not like animals?'

You are right.

Animals are cute.

Animals are furry and some *are* bacon-flavoured.

BUT animals are also ancient killing machines who want to learn how to use woks so they can kill us all and eat our livers and kidneys in a tasty and nutritious stir-fry.

There are three other reasons I do not like animals.

1. Octopuses are much smarter than humans, they are super strong and have six more arms than us. The only reason octopuses haven't taken over the world yet is that they are really, very, super disorganised. Last week I finished a book by Dr Erich von Odet Jnr called *The octopuses are getting organised and will take over the world and make us all their slaves! Soon!* The book said that the octopuses are getting organised and will take over the world and make us all their slaves. Soon! It contained several very convincing charts.

WHAT THE SUPER-INTELLIGENT OCTOPUSES WILL BE CAPABLE OF NOW THEY ARE GETTING ORGANISED

- Fighting seven humans while doing a Sudoku.
- Cooking eight human liver and kidney stir-fries.
- Cooking four human liver and kidney stir-fries, fighting three people and doing a Sudoku.
- Washing the dishes really quickly and thoroughly.

2. You know those tiny, fluffy dogs that some ladies keep in their handbags? Well those dogs were once wolves! All dogs were once wolves! That means that some ladies are keeping tiny wolves in their handbags.
3. Llamas are fireproof.

When the super-intelligent organised octopuses team up with the handbag wolves and the fireproof llamas, we humans will be in a lot of trouble.

• • •

By the time we arrived at the llama farm, the bus smelled of bum-stink, air-freshener-stink and Townes McFarlane's vomit.

• • •

The bus turned off the main road and stopped at a gate.

The gate was covered in signs.

The bus driver got out of the bus and opened the gate. She got back in the bus, drove through the gate and kept on driving. She didn't stop to close the gate.

Maybe the gate needs another sign.

The bus bounced down a long, pot-holed dirt driveway—past a wide, flat house with hundreds of

pairs of gumboots sitting on the back porch—and stopped in front of an enormous, rickety, wooden shed. Hardly any bits of the shed seemed to be touching each other. It looked like it was being held up by strings—like a marionette—and if someone let go of the strings, the whole thing would flop down in a heap.

We all squeezed off the bus. Waiting for us was the farmer. He had really skinny arms, really skinny legs, a huge belly and huge hands. His red-checked shirt was much too small for him. Most of the buttons wouldn't do up and you could see that his chest was covered in vast curls of woolly, grey hair. It looked like he was hiding a sheep down the front of his shirt.

'Ah . . . yeah . . . ah . . . gidday,' said the farmer. 'Ummmmm . . . yeah . . . righto . . . umm . . . dinner . . . ah . . . yeah . . . will . . . be at dinnertime . . . righto . . . ah . . . look around . . . if youse like . . . ummm . . . unless . . . ah . . . yeah . . . you're blind then . . . ummm . . . maybe . . . feel around . . . ah . . . yeah . . . sorry . . . yeah . . . no . . . I didn't . . . ummm . . . mean to . . . ummmmm . . . yeah . . . righto.'

The farmer turned around and walked back towards the house.

He had a very strange walk. Like he was hiding a sheep down the front of somewhere else as well.

• • •

'Attention,' said Mrs Whyte-Wale.

No one gave her their attention.

'Simon,' said Mrs Whyte-Wale.

Simon Bolivar screamed. (See? I told you he screams whenever anything happens to him.)

That got our attention.

'Thank you, Simon,' said Mrs Whyte-Wale. 'Once you have ALL taken your bags to the farmhouse and unpacked, find a buddy and you may explore the farm until dinnertime.'

'Hils?' I said. 'Do you want to be my buddy?'

She didn't answer.

'Hils?'

Hils had disappeared.

Hils disappears a lot.

REASONS HILS HAS GIVEN ME WHEN SHE HAS DISAPPEARED IN THE PAST

- 'I was gathering intelligence for an important mission.'
- 'None of your business.'
- 'I was attending a My Little Pony convention.'
- 'I didn't disappear! Everyone else disappeared. I stayed exactly where I was.'
- 'Don't make me silence you.'

• • •

After I had taken my bag over to the farmhouse, unpacked and pretended I had found a buddy, I started exploring the farm.

I walked around the back of the shed. There was some amazing stuff behind the shed. Hils would have loved it.

Thing I found around the back of the shed	Original purpose	What Hils probably would have used it for
Enormous rusty circular saw blade.	Sawing enormous logs.	A booby trap called The Silent Swinging Saw of Sudden Slicing.
A bale of rusty barbed wire.	Stopping llamas escaping.	A booby trap called The Bloody Bobbing Bale of Barbed Bereavement.
A huge, rusty spring with one really, very, super pointy end.	No idea.	A booby trap called The Pulsating Pointy Prong of Puncturing Panic.
A sheep's skull.	Holding in a sheep's brain.	A pot-plant holder.
A box full of rusty nails.	Nailing things.	A booby trap called The Nasty Nipping Nail of Noxious Nobbling.
A sort of box thingy where you pump a handle on the side and the top of the box moves down and crushes whatever is inside the box.	Making tomato juice.	Making orange juice. (Hils doesn't like tomato juice.)

Behind the behind-the-shed was a high, thick hedge. I walked alongside it until I got to an old wooden gate that was wet and dark and covered in moss.

That's when I saw them.

The llamas.

They were facing away from me so, at first, I didn't know they were llamas. I thought they were tall sheep who had lost a lot of weight and been working out at the gym.

I accidentally bumped the gate. It made a wet CLOMMMM sort-of sound.

All the llamas turned around at the same time and glared at me.

Before coming to the llama farm school camp I had done some research on llamas.

I knew llamas were fireproof.

I knew llamas have been around for about 40 million years.

I knew the Incas called them 'silent brothers' and used to worship them.

I knew that if you upset a llama they'd spit on you.

I knew llamas were quick learners.

I didn't know that llamas had such piercing glares.

The llamas were glaring at me the same way that my science teacher Mr Base-Ball glares at Evan de la Souza when Evan farts in class and blames it on Michelangelo the axolotl.

The llamas kept on glaring at me.

'Hils?' I said.

Hils did not miraculously appear like I had hoped she would.

The llamas kept on glaring.

'Stop it!' I said.

The llamas didn't stop it.

'You know it's rude to glare at someone, don't you?'

The llamas obviously didn't know it was rude because they just kept on glaring.

'Don't be so rude and . . . dumb!' I said.

The llamas glared.

'You're just dumb! Did you hear me? Dumb! Stop glaring! I am a human! I am superior to you! You shouldn't glare at your superiors. Stop thinking I'm not superior. I am superior! I invented the . . . umm . . . ahhh . . . I . . . invented . . . the . . . umm . . . flute. Yes! I invented the flute. You could never have thought of that. You couldn't even pick up a flute! Ha! Take that! I should say that I, Charlie Ian Duncan, *didn't invent* the flute. It was someone else. But they *were* a human just like me. They might have been my cousin. Whoever they were they weren't a rude, glary llama. No, they most certainly weren't. I don't have any cousins who are llamas. I don't even care if you're fireproof. Lots of things are fireproof. Like flutes. Well, if the flute is made out of fireproof stuff then it is fireproof. So there. You don't scare me. Even if you do form an alliance with octopuses and tiny, fluffy handbag wolves. I'm not scared of you! If I was I wouldn't show it anyway! Stop glaring! Stop it! Dumb llamas! You're so dumb! I'm going now because I don't like to be around such dumb llamas who can't even invent a flute. I am a human! I am your master! Stop it! Stop it!'

I turned and ran back towards the bus.

'I left my flute on the bus!' I said over my shoulder to the llamas as I kept on running.

I knew they were still glaring at me.

I just knew it.

• • •

After dinner at the farmhouse we all had to go out to the shed where we were going to have a group discussion about the ecosystem of the farm.

'Charlie?' said Mrs Whyte-Wale as I was trudging towards the shed. 'Have you seen Hilary? She wasn't at dinner.'

Hils hates being called Hilary.

'She's sick,' I said. 'She went to bed early.'

'Oh, all right,' said Mrs Whyte-Wale. 'I'm sure she'll be better in the morning.'

Hils was not sick. Hils had not gone to bed early. I didn't know where Hils was.

I was worried about Hils.

I wanted to know where

WHY MRS WHYTE-WALE WASN'T MORE CONCERNED ABOUT WHERE HILS WAS

It's because Mrs Whyte-Wale doesn't like Hils. I always thought that teachers were meant to like all their pupils. Well they don't. I guess it's fair enough. Hils doesn't like Mrs Whyte-Wale.

she was. What if the llamas had kidnapped her? Do llamas kidnap people? I was sure it wouldn't be a good idea to abduct Hils. She could beat any llamas that tried to kidnap her. *Could* she beat any llamas that tried to kidnap her? Maybe not. Surely I would have known if the llamas had tried to abduct Hils. She would have said something like, 'Help! The llamas are trying to abduct me!' Wait a minute! Hils would never say 'Help!' Never ever. Not even in a 100% 'Help!' situation. Maybe the llamas knew that Hils would never say 'Help! no matter what and that made her the perfect target?

I didn't know what to think.

Not knowing what to think is really confusing.

Also, why was Mrs Whyte-Wale sure that Hils would be better in the morning? Mrs Whyte-Wale isn't a doctor. She is an English teacher. English teachers aren't doctors. If English teachers were doctors we'd probably all get flesh-eating disease and die.

• • •

Our group discussion about the ecosystem of the farm was exactly as boring as I thought it was going to be.

• • •

Mr Base-Ball turned off the light in the boys' bedroom. I closed my eyes and tried to go to sleep but I couldn't.

I was worried about Hils.

And it was too quiet.

I didn't know that farms were so quiet at night.

At night my house is never this quiet.

My house creaks. Like it's yawning. Tired after a long day of having a roof. Having a roof *would* be really tiring.

At home, every time my parents turn off the hot tap in the kitchen there's an almighty THOMB sound in the bathroom. At half past nine every night something thumps onto our roof. It does worry me a bit but it's been going on for ages now and I haven't been murdered so I figure it's not a murderer. I hear cars go past my house. I hear bikes go past my house. Once, I heard something go past my house that sounded like a dolphin riding a skateboard that had tin cans for wheels.

Here it was so quiet. Too quiet.

There had to be *some* noise.

I listened really hard.

I could hear *some* noise.

It sounded like something with really loud nostrils trying to breathe quietly. While chewing something crunchy without making a crunching sound. While walking around softly in tap-dancing shoes.

I listened carefully. I realised what the sound was.

It was the llamas.

I could hear the llamas.

They were not not-breathing. They were not not-chewing. They were not not-tap-dancing.

They were talking.

They were having a discussion.

And I knew exactly what they were discussing. They were discussing me.

This was all my fault. I should have played it cool. But I hadn't. I had let the llamas know that I knew all about them. That I knew they were fireproof. That I knew they didn't invent the flute.

Wait a minute!

What if they didn't know about the octopuses?

What if they didn't know about the handbag wolves?

I'd just told them all about them.

Now they knew. Now they might get in contact with the octopuses and handbag wolves and form

an alliance. What would that alliance do first? Get rid of me that's what. They'd have to get rid of me because I was onto them. I knew the llamas, octopuses and handbag wolves were in cahoots. They'd have to silence me. That's what I would do.

Oh no! All those things out the back of the shed. The llamas, octopuses and handbag wolves could use that stuff to make some sort of thing to silence me.

I bet they'd make a flute.

A Death Flute.

A Flute of Death.

A Death Flute of Death.

Calm down, Charlie.

Breathe.

Think.

That was better.

Right, I had to do something.

I had to stop the llamas getting in touch with the octopuses and handbag wolves and making a Death Flute of Death.

I should have cut the phone lines! That'd be no use. The llamas probably have mobile phones.

What was I going to do?

What was I going to do?

What was I going to do?

Evan de la Souza farted in his sleep.

'It was Michelangelo,' he said in a way-too-loud-sleep-talking voice.

• • •

I walked out the back door onto the porch and slipped my feet into one of the hundred pairs of gumboots. It felt funny wearing gumboots with no socks. Like my feet had decided I was a nudist but they hadn't told the rest of me.

• • •

I stumbled towards the shed in the dark. (Farm dark is a lot darker than town dark.) The little moonlight there was made everything look like one of those glowing deepsea fish. I walked around the back of the shed expecting to see a Giant Rusty Spring Eel, an Enormous Saw-blade Ray and a Sheep Skull Shark.

But none of those things were there.

I looked for the box of rusty nails. Gone.

I looked for the box thingy. Gone.

The barbed wire. Gone.

No, no, no, no, no, no, no. The llamas had all that stuff.

They'd probably already built the Death Flute of Death.

I ran to the gate. The llamas were there.

'I'm sorry. I'm really sorry,' I said. 'We got off on the wrong foot. Please don't death me with the Death Flute of Death. I won't tell on you. I'll even give you the octopuses' phone number so you can call them and form a cahoots with them if you haven't already. I don't think you can't do it. I don't think you're dumb. I know I said I did but I don't.'

'Maintain radio silence!' said one of the llamas.

'Maintain radio silence' is the army way of saying 'be quiet'.

'Oh, I'm sorry,' I said.

Then I realised that a llama had just spoken to me.

I don't often scream but I felt that being spoken to by a llama was exactly the sort of situation which called for a scream.

A really big scream.

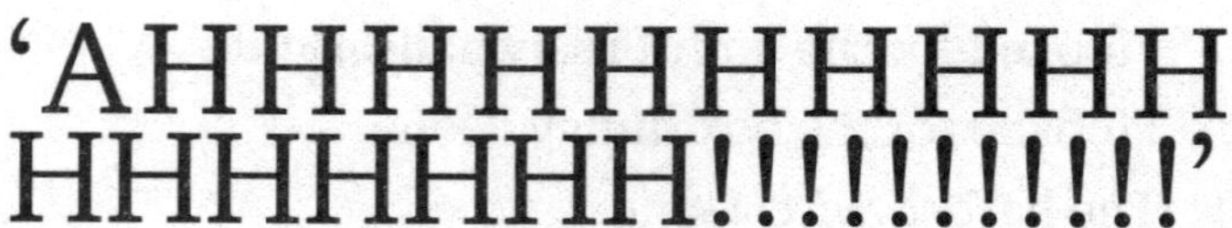

‘Maintain radio silence!’ said the llama.

‘AHHHHHHHHHHHHHHHHHH!!!!!!!!!!!’

‘Why do you continue to disobey my direct orders?’ said the llama which, now I thought about it, sounded quite a lot like Hils.

I looked closely at the llama.

It was either an actual llama or else Hils had made an amazing llama costume out of a sheepskin, an old cardigan, a feather duster, two bananas, one dark brown Ugg boot, four yoghurt containers, a plastic bag full of onions and a funnel.

‘Excuse me, but are you a llama or Hils?’

‘I am Hils.’

‘I thought you were a llama,’ I said.

‘That’s exactly what I wanted you to think,’ said Hils.

‘Why?’

‘Strategically this farm is not safe. If insurgents wished to mount an attack on us they would be able to do it from at least three sides. I have spent the last eight hours building defences to protect both

our flanks and have disguised myself as a llama to protect our rear.'

'Is that why the saw blade and nails and crushy box thingy are missing? Have you used them?'

'Affirmative.'

'To make a Death Flute of Death?'

'Negative. I have no idea what a Death Flute of Death is,' said Hils.

'Why have you done all this, Hils? We're not going to be attacked from the flank or the rear. We're on a school camp. At a llama farm. School camps at llama farms don't get attacked.'

Just then is when we were attacked.

A bright light blinded Hils and me at the same time as we were deafened by a really, very, super loud air-horn.

'GIDDAY,' said a voice through a really, very, super loud megaphone. 'WE HEARD YOU SCREAMING. YOU ARE NOW SURROUNDED BY FARM FORCE! CEASE AND DESIST EVERYTHING YOU ARE DOING. PUT YOUR HANDS UP. YOU'RE UNDER ARREST. RIGHTO.'

'Run,' said Hils.

When Hils tells you to run you should just run. Straight away. However, I think all people in positions of power must be held accountable for their actions. So I didn't run *straight away*.

'Why?' I said.

'I'm about to activate all of the defences I spent the last eight hours building.'

I decided not to run. I wanted to see Hils' defences in action.

• • •

Hils had made some really, very, super great defences.

A giant, rusty saw-blade arced noiselessly across the sky, causing all the members of Farm Force to throw themselves down onto the ground.

'Hils?' I said. 'Is that a Silent Swinging Saw of Sudden Slicing?'

'Negative,' said Hils.

The Farm Forcers shouted and squealed as a big, tangled ball of rusty barbed wire bounced across the ground towards them.

'That must be a Bloody Bobbing Bale of Barbed Bereavement,' I said.

'Negative.'

When a huge spring with one really pointy end started ricocheting all over the place, sending the

Farm Forcers scrambling for cover, I didn't ask Hils whether it was a Pulsating Pointy Prong of Puncturing Panic. I knew it was.

'Should we run now?' I said to Hils.

'Affirmative.'

• • •

I crawled back into bed and closed my eyes.

Hils' defences were still defencing Farm Force so there was a lot more noise going on outside than there had been.

WHOOSH.

'Watch out!'

CHANK. CHANK. CHANK. CHANK.

'Behind you!'

FLIMMMMMMMMM.

'I've been nipped! And nobbled! By something noxious!'

PHIT. PHIT. PHIT. PHIT. PHIT. PHIT. PHIT.

'Retreat! Farm Force retreat!'

'I've lost a gumboot! I'm going back for it!'

'Don't be a fool!'

HOOOOOOOOOOOOOOOOOOOOOOOOOO.

'No! A flying pot-plant holder!'

'Ahhhhhhhhhhhhhhhhhhh!'

It sounded a lot more like town now.

I fell asleep almost straight away.

ABOUT THE AUTHORS

Andy Griffiths

Andy Griffiths is one of Australia's most popular children's authors. From his bestselling, award-winning Treehouse series to the JUST! books (both series illustrated by Terry Denton) and *The Day My Bum Went Psycho*, Andy's books have captivated Australian kids for more than twenty years. His books have been *New York Times* bestsellers, adapted for the stage and television and won more than 50 Australian children's choice awards. Andy, a passionate advocate for literacy, is an ambassador for The Indigenous Literacy Foundation and The Pyjama Foundation.

What makes me laugh are stupid jokes that aren't even funny, like this one:

Q: Why did the boy fall off his bike?

A: Because his mother threw a fridge at him.

And this one:

Two penguins are standing on an iceberg. One turns to the other and says, 'Radio'.

Did I just annoy you with these stupid jokes that aren't even funny? I hope so. Because the thought that I've annoyed you by telling you stupid jokes that aren't even funny also makes me laugh.

Frances Watts

Frances Watts was born in Switzerland and grew up in Australia. Her bestselling picture books include *Goodnight, Mice!* (ill. Judy Watson), winner of the 2012 Prime Minister's Award for Children's Fiction; 2006 CBCA Honour Book *Kisses for Daddy* (ill. David Legge); and 2008 Children's Book Council of Australia award-winner *Parsley Rabbit's Book about Books* (ill. David Legge). Frances is also the author of the fantasy/adventure series the Gerander Trilogy and the Sword Girl series (ill. Gregory Rogers), as well as two YA novels: *The Raven's Wing*, set in Ancient Rome, and *The Peony Lantern*, set in nineteenth-century Japan.

www.franceswatts.com

Frances Watts is a very serious person. She doesn't like jokes or games or puzzles or pranks or quips or riddles, and she never laughs. Except at cheese. She thinks cheese is hilarious. Also lobsters.

Morris Gleitzman

Morris Gleitzman is a bestselling Australian children's author. His books explore serious and sometimes confronting subjects in humorous and unexpected ways. His titles include *Two Weeks With The Queen*, *Grace*, *Doubting Thomas*, *Bumface*, *Give Peas A Chance*, *Extra Time*, *Loyal Creatures* and the series *Once*, *Then*, *Now*, *After* and *Soon*. Morris lives in Sydney and Brisbane, and his books are published in more than twenty countries.

I never know what makes me laugh till I see or hear it. That's one of the things about humour, it works best when it catches you by surprise. But I can say that people who stay optimistic and hopeful against the odds always make me smile. And some of the best moments of humour for me have tears close by.

Katrina Nannestad

Katrina Nannestad grew up in country New South Wales in a neighbourhood stuffed full of happy children. Her adult years have been spent teaching, travelling, raising boys, perfecting her recipe for chocolate-chip bickies and pursuing her love of stories.

Katrina celebrates family, friendship and belonging in her writing. She also loves creating stories that make children laugh. What can be better than contagious belly giggles, hen-like cackles or wild guffaws that end in a snort? Her books include *The Girl Who Brought Mischief*, the winner of the 2014 NSW Premier's Award for Children's Literature, the Patricia Wrightson Prize; *Bungaloo Creek;* the Red Dirt Diary series; and the Olive of Groves series.

Katrina now lives in country Victoria with her family and an exuberant black whippet called Olive. She dreams of one day owning a spotted pig called Harold.

There's so much funny stuff out there! Animals crack me up—especially pigs, turkeys and tapirs. To me, they seem almost human and I love to imagine the things they might be thinking and saying. Bare bottoms, banana peels and bagpipes all make me giggle. Words do, too. 'Flummoxed', 'pithy' and 'pudding' are all rippers.

But the one thing that makes me laugh every day, without fail, is my whippet, Olive. She pretends to be a gentle little lady if she wants a treat or a cuddle, but chases her tail like a whirlwind when she thinks no one is looking. She's scared of kittens, babies and carpet fluff, but fearless when it comes to horses and bulls. She also bites her fingernails—or are they toenails? I'm not sure, but it's funny.

Tony Wilson

Tony Wilson is the author of the bestselling *The Cow Tripped over the Moon* which was a CBCA Honour Book in 2016. He's written for adults and kids, and his latest titles are *Emo the Emu* and *The Selwood Boys*.

www.tonywilson.com.au

I've never been great at laughing at jokes. There's too much pressure. As soon as the joke teller starts the joke, I get a bit panicky that maybe I won't find the joke funny, and worry that I'll have to pretend to laugh at the end of the joke. This distracts me from actually enjoying the joke, so I normally have to pretend to laugh at the end of the joke.

There are things that genuinely make me laugh, though. These include penguins, kids shooting too fast off the bottom of slides, people walking into things while staring at mobile phones, toddlers chucking tantrums in supermarkets, giraffes, baboons, cricketers getting hit in the box, and my four children: Polly, Harry, Jack and Alice.

Sally Rippin

Sally Rippin was born in Darwin, but grew up mainly in South-East Asia. As a young adult she lived in China for three years, studying traditional Chinese painting. Sally has over sixty books published, many of them award-winners. Her most recent work includes the highly acclaimed children's novel *Angel Creek* and the popular *Billie B Brown* books, which became the highest selling series for 6-8 year olds in Australia within the first year of their release. In 2015, Sally was Australia's highest selling female author and her *Billie B Brown* books have sold more than 2.5 million copies since first published. Sally presents in schools and at literary festivals both in Australia and overseas, and has a regular program on 3RRR interviewing children's authors and industry professionals. She is a passionate ambassador for the *100 Story Building* creative writing centre for marginalized youth. She and her partner co-founded *Story Peddlers,* a hand-made performance tent that packs away into a custom-built bike, with the aim of bringing back the art of the roving storyteller.

What makes me laugh is people with no self-awareness, like Aunt Thelma. People who think they are really rather special when they're not. The people I like the most are the ones who don't try to be anything other than who they are. Like monkeys. When did you last see a monkey pretend to be something other than a monkey, right? Monkeys are the best. I wish I'd had a monkey when I was growing up. But then again, my two younger sisters were pretty funny, too.

Jaclyn Moriarty

Jaclyn Moriarty grew up in Sydney, lived in the US, the UK and Canada, and now lives in Sydney again. She is the author of the Ashbury–Brookfield books (including *Feeling Sorry for Celia* and *Finding Cassie Crazy*) and the Colours of Madeleine trilogy (*A Corner of White, The Cracks in the Kingdom* and *A Tangle of Gold*). Her novels are published internationally and have won many prizes.

Laughter that falls onto me from the sky comes from the funny things my ten-year-old says. ('You look so young!' he told me once. 'Or you *would* anyway, if it wasn't for all the wrinkly bits.') (That also made me cry a bit.)

Or when my small nephew asked his mother, 'Can we get a cat?'

'No, I'm sorry,' she replied. 'I'm allergic to cats.'

'That's okay,' he said. 'Just don't eat it.'

Meg McKinlay

Meg McKinlay writes picture books, novels, poetry, fragments of randomness, and anything else that drops into her head out of the clear blue sky. She lives near the ocean in Fremantle, Western Australia, where clear blue sky is very easy to come by. She is always finding faces in things but is yet to stumble across a Bieber.

Things that make her laugh include: wordplay, people who worship burnt toast, and the sight of her own face first thing in the morning. Her favourite joke is: 'Sticks float. They wood.' If you don't find this hilarious, you cannot be her friend.

Alan Brough

Alan Brough was born in New Zealand and is quite a bit older than he'd like to be. Alan has always loved books and, from an early age, wanted to be a writer. Then he and his Dad went to see Star Wars and Alan decided that, actually, he really, really, really, really, really wanted to be an actor.

After having been an actor for a while Alan realised there wasn't that much work for a 6-foot 4-inch guy with a slightly lopsided face and thick curly hair so he tried his hand at directing, broadcasting, composing, dancing (true!), singing and, in an unexpected turn of events, being a professional music nerd.

Recently, he got around to being a writer.

One day he hopes to have a bio that includes phrases like 'bestselling', 'award-winning' and 'so successful that he recently bought a solid-gold toilet' but, until then, he's just happy to look at his copy of *Charlie and the War Against the Grannies* and think, 'Cool! I wrote a book!'

What makes me laugh more than anything else is little kids swearing. Really little kids. Kids that have only recently started to talk. There's just something about a toddler saying a rude word in their gorgeous little voice. If you have a little brother or sister get them to do it. You'll see what I mean.

ABOUT THE ILLUSTRATOR

Andrea Innocent

Andrea Innocent began professionally illustrating after returning from living in Japan in 2006. Her personal illustrations tell stories of Japanese ghosts, folktales and depict quirky newspaper articles. Her commercial work covers many areas from editorial illustration to animation. Clients include Microsoft, The Melbourne Recital Centre, Malvern Star, *Rolling Stone Magazine*, *The Australian* and *The Age*. She is also a member of The Jacky Winter Group in Melbourne.

Andrea has also given talks and workshops on all sorts of topics related to illustration and design, such as professional practice, drawing, marketing and character design. She also teaches part-time.

She is currently working from her home studio in the hills with her partner, infant son, elderly cat and her Welsh Cardigan Corgi 'Pickles McGerkin'.

www.andreainnocent.com

What makes me laugh are sports mascots, particularly Japanese baseball characters. It's something about the enormous head, usually being held up by tiny, comical looking arms and the completely uncoordinated way they run around and into things. That's what makes me laugh, that and making food into a face :-).

THE
END